D0160346

Girlwood

Girlwood

By Claire Dean

illustrated by Aya Kato

Houghton Mifflin Company
Boston 2008

Definitions of herbal plants derived from Gregory L. Tilford, *Edible and Medicinal Plants of the West* (Missoula, Montana: Mountain Press, 1997)

www.houghtonmifflinbooks.com

The text of this book is set in Centaur MT.
The illustrations are pen and ink.

Library of Congress Cataloging-in-Publication
Dean, Claire.
Girlwood / By Claire Dean.
p. cm.

Summary: When Polly Greene's older sister Bree runs away from home, Polly and her
eccentric grandmother believe she is hiding in the neighboring Idaho woods, and when
they discover a mysterious, hidden grove of larches, Polly and her friends build a shelter
for Bree and try to save the grove from developers.

ISBN-13: 978-0-618-88390-5
[1. Conservation of natural resources—Fiction. 2. Runaways—Fiction. 3.
Grandmothers—Fiction. 4. Nature—Fiction. 5. Idaho—Fiction.] I. Title.

PZ7.D3438Gi 2008
[Fic]—dc22
2007034265

Manufactured in the United States of America
MP 10 9 8 7 6 5 4 3 2 1

For my beautiful
daughter,
without whom
this book would
not exist

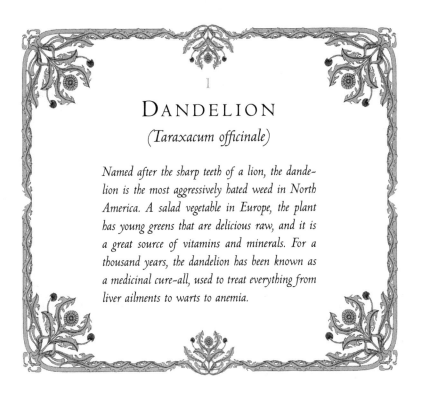

DANDELION

(Taraxacum officinale)

*Named after the sharp teeth of a lion, the dande-
lion is the most aggressively hated weed in North
America. A salad vegetable in Europe, the plant
has young greens that are delicious raw, and it is
a great source of vitamins and minerals. For a
thousand years, the dandelion has been known as
a medicinal cure-all, used to treat everything from
liver ailments to warts to anemia.*

The first and last kiss Polly received from her sister was as
contrary as Bree herself. Lightweight but intense, a kiss that
was supposed to impart some deep meaning but offer zero
affection, a kiss that was retracted nearly before it began. It
was past midnight, and Polly was not only too tired to open
her eyes, she was so sick of her stoned, skeletal, sixteen-year-
old sister that she didn't even acknowledge Bree was there.

It was just like Bree to ruin Polly's favorite hour, the only time she had left to swim with mermaids or imagine herself flying without Bree asking her if she was having some kind of fit. Polly kept her eyes shut tight and pictured a magical woodland creature instead of her sister, the flutter of a fairy's kiss instead of Bree's.

She stuck to this vision, even when the fairy didn't smell like cedar or honeysuckle but like an unwashed teenager and marijuana smoke. The kiss was even more far-fetched than fairies, if you asked Polly. It had been months since Bree had entered Polly's room except to steal cash. In fact, Polly couldn't remember the last time her sister had said anything to her aside from "Shut up" or "Freak" or, when Polly had caught her snorting up a line of white powder, "If you tell Mom, I'll kill you."

🌿 🌿 🌿 🌿

Not too long ago, things had been different. Bree had been the pretty, pampered, delicate one, the blond-haired, blue-eyed doll, and Polly her younger, tougher, dirtier accomplice. The four-year age difference hadn't seemed so important then, since they both liked to draw and dance and, mostly, play in the woods behind their house. Beneath the solemn pines and flashy cottonwoods, Bree crowned herself princess of the green kingdom and made Polly her woodland fairy—

the one who must constantly be on guard to save her sister from dragons, trolls, and other assorted dangers. Polly never minded. She was strong, and Bree was beautiful. They each had their place.

But then Bree turned sixteen, and declared such games pathetic. The new Evil Bree stopped talking to Polly entirely and hid like a mole in her dark bedroom, coming out only when their mom confronted her with the pills she'd found in her coat pocket or when Aaron Sykes showed up.

Bree braved daylight for her boyfriend, maybe because Aaron Sykes brought a cloud with him everywhere he went. He wore all black and had a halo of darkness around his head that stretched even farther, a bleakness that gave Polly the creeps. He mumbled and smelled funny, and Polly's parents said they didn't trust him, which instantly made Bree love him more.

As soon as she started dating him, Bree began to dress like Aaron, hold her cigarette between her thumb and forefinger the way he did, sample his favorite drugs. It took no time at all to complete her transformation from girl to Aaron's shadow, as if love wasn't measured in goodness and devotion but in how much you'd give up for a person, how far you'd sink.

❧ ❧ ❧ ❧

At least the bottom came quickly. Three months after they started going out, Aaron dumped Bree for another girl-shadow, and Bree came home in tears. Trembling, inconsolable, Bree became the princess in need of saving again, except that now Polly couldn't help her anymore, and she didn't want to. They might have been sisters, but Bree had made it clear they were going it alone.

Polly's mother said, "Thank God," but in truth after the breakup things only got worse. Bree may have lost the boyfriend but she kept his bad habits. She still wore black, ditched school, took even riskier drugs, like she was *really* proving her love now, disintegrating over someone who didn't even want her. Evil Bree was still pretty as a doll, but the horror-film kind—an inanimate object that comes to life for the sole purpose of destroying everything.

Now the mattress hardly budged as Bree sat on the bed. After Aaron, she had started losing weight. Down, down, down, like Alice through the rabbit hole, until she was a hundred pounds, starting to grow fur like an animal fighting to keep warm, and suddenly popular. Her phone rang day and night; even thugs like Brad Meyer called to ask her out. Now that Bree was bent on destroying herself, she was apparently a girl worth getting to know.

- *4* -

"Polly?"

Polly peeked out through half-closed lids when the fairy began to cry. Bree clasped a handful of dandelion stems, their puffy white seeds long gone now that fall had come on. Maybe she'd listened to their grandmother after all and knew that instead of banishing dandelions from the lawn, you could eat the delicious young leaves or cure almost anything with the milky juice in the root.

Polly said nothing. There were no words left except cruel ones, and Polly had said all of those.

"Polly?" the fairy said once more. "You know when you love someone, you think they'll never hurt you? It's not true, Polly. When Aaron left me, I wished I'd died."

Polly squeezed her eyes shut again. She wished she could shut her ears, too. She didn't want to hear this. Didn't Bree get that? It was like Bree kept dragging her onto a roller coaster she wasn't tall enough to ride.

Think of fairies, Polly thought. *Imagine the one on the bed flying away.*

And that was exactly what happened. Polly felt a brush of wind, a stiff, damaged wing against her cheek, and then . . . nothing.

"I'm leaving," the fairy said from across the room. "Don't tell Mom until you have to, all right? I'll be somewhere in the woods. *Our* woods. I've got to try to be all right."

It was a dream for sure. The northern Idaho woods were a vast forest, and Bree was miles from all right.

Polly opened her eyes in time to see the fairy skimming across the hardwood floor, stirring up the gauzy curtains with her wings. She walked to the door, dandelions in hand, a red glow swirling around her middle. Aaron Sykes wasn't the first person with a halo Polly had spotted. All her life she'd seen the light and colors around living things. When people laughed, spikes of yellow, orange, and blue shot up from their heads. Dogs looped their shadows around the people they loved. Even roses had an aura—every winter, they were covered with spectral blossoms right where the flowers would bloom in spring.

She had thought everyone saw these things until the day, a year ago, when she confided in Bree. Her sister had looked at the empty space above Polly's head and called her visions psycho stuff. "They'll lock you up for saying things like that," she said.

Now the red glow around the fairy looked like blood, like damage that couldn't be undone. Bree's jeans were so loose they had to be tied around her fragile hips with a double-looped belt. She paused at the door.

"I love you, Polly," she said, and because it was such a far-fetched dream to begin with, Polly didn't scoff or point out all the things that Bree had ruined.

"Love you too, Bree," she said. "Bye."

JUNIPER
(Juniperus)

Growing abundantly in the wild, many Juniper species have also been domesticated. Juniper berries can be ground for use in sauces, crushed like peppercorns, and are the primary ingredient in gin. Medicinally, the berries aid digestion and relieve stomach ailments, while the smoke has been used for purification and to improve clairvoyance.

In the morning when her alarm rang to wake her for school, Polly was groggy. She knew she'd dreamed again, but all she could remember were mermaids and fairies, images Bree would say were further evidence of a disturbed mind. Since her father had moved out three months ago, Polly had had trouble sleeping. Her dad once told her that he'd tuck her in until she was eighteen, and there was no way she could stop him. But maybe divorce was the loophole, the way out of promises he'd never planned to keep.

Obviously, he hadn't planned to finish his story, either—the one he'd told to her every night for seven years, ever since she was five and swore that there were fairies in the woods behind their house.

"The woods were still in danger," he'd said the last time he tucked her in. He was such a big man—his head skimming low ceilings, his body thick and solid as a tree trunk—her entire mattress slanted when he sat and she rolled right into him.

"Whole groves of trees were dying of some mysterious disease," he continued. "And so was Gwendolyn, the woodland fairy. If she couldn't find her way to the heart of the wild woods, to Fairyland, she would die."

Polly gripped the blanket. "She had to go to the Dark Lands, didn't she?" she whispered.

Her father nodded grimly. "Yes. The only place she hadn't searched. The place she had assumed could never hold Fairyland because it was so dark, so awful."

The next day, her dad had packed his things and moved to a rustic cabin in the woods, and the story Polly had thought was never-ending ended there. She could think of a dozen solutions to Gwendolyn's problems, but she wanted her dad to tell her which one was the truth.

Now Polly trudged into the hall where Bree's door, with its NO TRESPASSING sign and handwritten *That means you, Polly,* was closed. She finally remembered last night's dream, but it seemed even more ludicrous in the light of day. Her mother would call it her "wild imagination," which was basically mom-speak for *freak*. Not that Polly wasn't used to people thinking her weird. Even in elementary school, the kids had spotted the dirt she tracked in from the woods and the way she looked above their heads when they laughed. By twelve, she was loser material.

Downstairs, Polly's mother stared out the kitchen window even though a hedge of cobweb-covered junipers blocked half the view. Polly's grandmother used juniper berries to ease stomachaches, while Polly's mom grew the plant because it required no care.

Her mom didn't hear her cross the room to the refrigerator. Faith Greene wore a tattered pink bathrobe that used to reach her ankles but now skimmed the floor. She'd gotten shorter since Polly's dad moved out—or she'd been standing taller before the divorce, Polly wasn't sure which. All Polly knew was that as Bree fell apart, her mom stitched everything else tighter together. She took on more responsibilities at work, headed up the neighborhood watch, repainted the kitchen cabinets white. She had ignored Polly's dad's unhappiness, even after he quit his successful law practice. When he took up wood-carving, she dusted around him and pressed her lips into a tight, restrained line. She was silent as the eye of a hurricane while she ransacked Bree's room, vacuumed up wood shavings, and told her friends not to worry, that her daughter was fine and her husband was just taking a little break.

It was almost a relief when the yelling started.

Polly's mom's hair—the frizzy brown catastrophe Polly had inherited—looked like a bird's nest, like something from outside. Polly had gotten a mixture of her parents' eyes, sort of hazel, sort of brown. Wishy-washy. With her straight blond hair and vibrant blue eyes, Bree didn't look like any of them. This used to make Bree cry, but lately it was the only thing that pleased her.

Polly opened the freezer, and her mother jumped at the noise. "For Pete's sake, Polly," she said, whirling around and holding a hand to her chest. "You could clear your throat or something."

Polly put a waffle in the toaster and turned the knob to 10. It drove her mother crazy when she ate her waffles black, but it wasn't like she could complain—at least one of her daughters was eating.

"Did you sleep well?" her mom asked.

Polly said nothing. She knew to keep her mouth shut, especially not to say anything like *Bree came into my room last night. She was a fairy, but now she's gone.* She couldn't make the words sound more grown up, and she didn't want to. An adult would not have mistaken Bree for a fairy. An adult would have called her a runaway first thing.

Smoke swirled up from the toaster. "Is your sister up yet?" her mom asked. She walked to the doorway, not waiting for an answer. "Brianna!" she yelled up the stairs. "Time for school! You were supposed to set your alarm!"

Goose bumps broke out along Polly's skin. It was so silent in the house, she heard the noises that usually go unnoticed —leaves swirling outside in the early autumn breeze, the frantic flutter of wings against the screen door, her own heart pounding.

"I don't believe this," her mom said. "One little thing. That's all I'm asking. Just get up on time. Is that so hard?"

"Mom?"

"She thinks the sun should come up later just to suit her. I'm trying to keep her alive, and I'm the villain. I'm telling you, Polly. That's it. I'm done."

Polly gripped the table as her mom marched upstairs, feeling weightless, almost like the fairy herself.

Let the dream be true. Let Bree be gone.

The instant Polly formed the thought, she wanted to take it back. She wasn't like that. Bree was the one who was like that. What kind of horrible trick would it be if she ended up like her sister, even when she wanted more than anything to be like somebody else?

Polly felt lightheaded as she listened to her mother's footsteps, followed by a shock of silence, then the panicked cries of "Bree? Bree!"

3

MALLOW

(Malva neglecta)

Two thousand years ago, Romans were advised to take a daily sip of mallow juice to prevent illness. The entire plant is edible, and the fruits taste somewhat like cheese, earning the plant the nickname "cheese weed." The roots are thick and sticky, good for skin irritations and respiratory ailments.

Polly's mom went from irritated to hysterical in an instant. It was Jekyll and Hyde stuff, like there'd been a monster lurking in Faith Greene this whole time. Her face tightened and twitched; she paced and cried and made phone calls and ran outside every time someone with blond hair walked by.

Everything happened at warp speed. Within an hour of finding Bree's bedroom empty, Polly's mom called the police department in Laramie, Idaho, pummeled Bree's friends for information, and contacted Laramie High in case Bree showed up in class wondering what all the fuss was about. While a neighbor drove out to Polly's dad's cabin, where her father had yet to install a phone, Polly and her mother searched Bree's room. Her mom seemed almost comforted when they came across the usual pot bags and cigarettes, but cried when they discovered the three things that weren't there: Bree's winter coat, though it was only late September; sneakers; and a ratty stuffed bear, a toy Bree hadn't touched in years.

The hour when Polly usually left for school came and went. She was perched on the edge of the living room sofa, still in her blue pajama bottoms and T-shirt, when her dad arrived. The laces on his boots were untied, his beard and hair wild, though he always looked that way now. He usually greeted Polly with a bear hug, but today he looked right past her toward her mother.

"What happened?" he asked. "Did you and Bree argue again?"

Polly's mom clutched the cordless phone to her chest, an odd, unsettling gesture, like she was cradling a baby. "Don't you dare blame this on me."

"I'm not blaming anyone. I need to know where my daughter is."

"I don't know! I've called everyone I can think of and no one's seen her. She ran away, or someone crawled in her window and took her."

Her dad paled. "My God. How can you say that?"

Polly couldn't stand to be in the same room with them anymore; it was like being poisoned. Her mom started to cry—guttural, bone-racking sobs that made Polly's hair stand on end.

※ ※ ※ ※

Officer Max Wendt showed up during what would have been Polly's second period, her debate class. He wore civilian clothes and would have been completely ordinary-looking were it not for the gun at his hip. He shook her dad's hand but steered clear of her mother, whose head had begun to bobble as if her whole body was coming loose. Polly imagined she'd soon see bolts flying, rusted nails and screws dropping to the floor.

They all knew Max Wendt: he was the one who was called out to Polly's grandmother's house whenever someone complained about the height of the weeds she called a garden or about the rough and desperate clientele who kept showing up at her door for her natural remedies. To Polly's grandmother, *natural* meant the extracts, oils, and teas she harvested from plants, like the mallow ointment she'd used last week to soothe Abby Gail's chicken pox. To many people in town, though, *natural* meant "bogus" or "illegal." To Pastor Bentley, Baba's remedies were the work of the devil, which made Baba laugh. When Polly's grandmother heard she was the centerpiece of the minister's sermon, she called herself a celebrity and cheered.

"We usually wait twenty-four hours before we do anything," Officer Wendt said, as they walked into the kitchen.

"Usually?" Polly's mom cried, grabbing his arm. "What do you mean, usually? You have to do something!"

The officer was a big man, probably six two, but he shrank from Faith Greene's frenzied face.

"We'll go to the school, talk to her friends," he offered.

Polly rolled her eyes. Bree's friends—the Fab Five, as they called themselves, though there was nothing fabulous about them unless you counted how good they all were at going up in flames—weren't big talkers. Like Bree, they used to be good girls; then the first fabulous one had shot up, and the rest had raced to keep up, as if they'd rather self-destruct than be left out. Bree acted like they cared more about her than her own family did, but where were the Fab Five now?

"I don't think you need to worry," the officer went on, gently extricating his arm. "Teenagers are always getting mad at their parents and making a dash for it. But then they've got to figure out the particulars, like how they'll eat, where they'll sleep. Your daughter will be walking through that door any minute. Mark my words."

They all looked at the front door, which didn't budge. Polly's mom started making weird sounds, noises well beyond crying.

"What about . . . abduction?" she asked. Polly's dad stood uncertainly in the doorway to the kitchen, as if he hadn't bought this house himself fifteen years ago.

"Faith," he said. "Stop it."

Polly's mom pressed a hand to her belly and moaned like she had a terrible stomachache. The policeman fixed his gaze on Polly, as if she were the only safe thing in the room.

"Was there any sign of struggle?" he asked. "Torn sheets? The window left open? Blood?"

Polly was about to respond when her mom said, "She hardly took anything. Just a jacket, a pair of shoes, a stuffed animal. Is that all runaways usually take?"

The officer looked away. "Let's not jump to any conclusions."

"She wouldn't just leave," Polly's dad said. "There must be an explanation."

They all shook their heads as if Bree were an angel, as if they'd forgotten who they were dealing with.

"She was trying to vanish into thin air," her mom said. She

was absolutely still for a moment, not even breathing. "Now she has."

Polly's teeth hurt, the way they did when she had a big test and had been grinding them in her sleep. She stepped forward.

"Bree's in the woods," she said.

For a moment, no one said anything. Her mom stared at her as if she couldn't understand a word she was saying. It was Max Wendt who finally broke the silence. "How do you know that?" he asked.

Polly fidgeted beneath his steady gaze. "I saw her last night. She said she was going to the woods and would try to be all right."

Her mother started moaning again while the policeman smiled at Polly the way adults often did, like she was darling and ridiculous.

"Ah," he said.

Her father tugged one of her curls. "Of course she'll be all right," he said. "But you're my wood sprite. You're the one who'd go into the woods, not Bree."

Polly couldn't argue. When Bree had turned sixteen and moved indoors, Polly continued to climb trees and make fairy villages out of twigs and mud. She still searched for the forest plants her grandmother said were edible—salty monkey flower leaves, miner's lettuce, the roots of the purple-flowered salsify that, remarkably, tasted like oysters from the sea. Polly was the only one who cried when it was announced that beginning this year much of the woods around town would be turned into a thousand-home subdivision called Mountain Winds.

"I know it doesn't sound right," Polly said to the officer. "But that's what Bree said. She's in the woods. All you have to do is look."

Max Wendt was still smiling condescendingly, but at least he said, "I'll send a couple men out there. If she did head into the woods, she couldn't have gotten far."

Polly didn't know if that was an insult or if he was just dumb. Even a girl like Bree could be miles away by now. She could be lost for good.

After the officer excused himself to search Bree's room, Polly's dad said, "It was probably just a dream, honey."

Polly widened her stance. "I saw her."

"I know what you think you saw," her dad replied. "Sometimes dreams can seem real. But—"

"I can find her," Polly said. "I know every inch of the woods."

She nearly made it to the door before something yanked her back by the hair. Her mom stood above her, her features so distorted she looked like someone Polly would avoid on the street. She twisted Polly's head to the side until Polly blinked back tears. For the first time in her life, she was afraid of her own mother.

"You can't go anywhere," her mom said. "Just . . . stay still. Don't move."

She released her grip slowly, as if Polly might bolt. But Polly's scalp throbbed so much she couldn't take a single step. Her mother had hurt her; she was hardly able to think.

Max Wendt came downstairs satisfied. "No signs of forced entry or foul play, but we'll get a detective out here just the same and send some men into the woods. I'll head down to the high school."

"I'll go with you," Polly's dad said.

Before they reached the front door, the knob turned.

"Bree?" Polly's mom said, flying across the room. The door opened wider, and Faith Greene's face fell at the sight of leather boots, a floor-length brown skirt, green camisole, and gray hair so long and wild it looked like a living thing.

Polly was the only one who smiled when she saw her grandmother. The policeman retreated a step, Polly's dad slipped out the door, and her mom collapsed on the sofa, her head in her hands.

The house filled with the scent of cedar, and Polly took a deep breath. Baba looked at each of them, then put her hands on her hips.

"What'd I miss?" she said.

4

TWISTED STALK

(Streptopus amplexifolius)

Found in shaded streambeds and moist areas across North America, the plant has young shoots and bright red, egg-shaped berries that taste like cucumbers and are an excellent trail snack. Also known as "scoot berries" for their laxative effect, the juice of the berries soothes minor burns and rashes.

By the afternoon, it was official: Brianna Greene had disappeared. Laramie, Idaho, was one of the fastest growing cities in the Northwest, a city of newcomers, a city of strangers, and Polly swore they were all in her house. People brought casseroles and fruit baskets and asked what they could do. They might have stayed for dinner if they hadn't noticed her grandmother standing at the kitchen stove, stirring a large pot of something unusually green and pungent.

When Baba fixed them with her stare, even the newest residents mumbled a quick goodbye and ran off as if they'd been hexed.

Baba smiled at Polly, her brown medicine bag slung around her neck. Every few minutes, she reached in the bag and pulled out a vial of crushed leaves or essential oils and added it to the pot. Slowly, the scent of the woods invaded the house, and Polly sat at the kitchen table and felt the knot in her shoulders finally beginning to relax. She was fairly certain that Baba added skullcap and valerian to the mixture, both strong herbal sedatives, but then around Baba, Polly always felt soothed.

"I saw her," Polly said.

Baba adjusted the heat on the stove and sat down. Her face was like one of those alluvial fans Polly had learned about in geography, a masterpiece of wrinkles and ridges. She was tall and slender, with arms still strong from chopping her own firewood and hair that fell to her waist. Polly's mother thought that Baba should have gone to the salon years ago, but then Polly's mom thought that everything about her own mother, from Baba's monthly bonfires to the way she helped women give birth beneath her purple ash tree, was inappropriate.

Polly, however, thought her grandmother was perfect. When Polly was young and had had trouble learning to speak, she called everything *baba*, from her grandma to her bottle to the trees. By the time the words came, she couldn't call her grandmother anything else. Baba *was* everything— laughter and calmness and the wisdom and abundance of the woods. Baba was the proof that you could be extraordinarily happy even if you were never liked.

"She came into my room last night," Polly went on. "She said she was going into the woods."

"Mm-hmmm."

"She had wings, like a fairy. Red around her middle. I've never seen that before."

Her grandma nodded, as if seeing auras were as normal as seeing stars. "Red's a battle color," Baba said. "Power and survival and often pain. You know what I've always said: when there's a problem, girls, run for the trees."

Polly heard her father's truck pass by the house. After getting nowhere at Bree's school, her dad had gone with Officer Wendt to talk to Aaron Sykes and Brad Meyer. Neither of them had any idea where Bree was. Aaron had been sleeping off another meth blitz when Bree disappeared and Brad hadn't seen Polly's sister for a week. Now Polly's dad was out driving around the neighborhood. Round and round and round.

"She can't survive," Polly said.

Baba gave her what most people call the witch's stare, the

one she fixed on anyone who came to her door for help, to see if they really wanted to get better or not. She didn't like to waste her time. "Why not? You'd survive, wouldn't you? You'd find shelter. You'd make fire the way I taught you, eat wild burdock and chickweed, even hunt if you had to." Baba paused and looked into the living room at Polly's mom. For a moment, her shoulders sagged, but when she turned back to Polly the heaviness was gone. "You'd do what others can't imagine, whatever is necessary," she went on. "That's what women always do."

"But it's all wrong! Bree's weak, and she hates the woods now."

Green, minty steam filled the room as the last neighbor left and Polly's mom slumped into the kitchen. She paused beside Baba's brew and wrinkled her nose. "I wish you wouldn't cook here," she said, leaning against the counter and massaging her forehead. "Everyone thinks Bree will be back before dawn."

Baba returned to her pot. "Hmmm."

"Hmmm what?" Polly's mother said, her Hyde face back. "What are you saying, Mom?"

"I'm saying if it wasn't fine when she left, how can it be fine when she comes home?" Baba asked. "Something has to change, and maybe it's Bree. I know you're terrified, Faith, but maybe Bree is doing exactly what she needs to do."

"Destroy me?" Polly's mom said. "That's what she needs to do?" She looked at Polly as if she wanted her to say something, side with her, but Polly didn't dare get between her mother and grandmother. It was a war zone in there, a no-woman's-land.

The only sound was the bubbling of Baba's potion until Polly's mom marched out of the room.

Baba sighed and turned back to her pot. Usually, Polly liked nothing better than to watch the light show around her grandmother—shimmery slivers of green rising from Baba's head and shoulders, like branches on a stately tree. Yet today, something was different. A few of those limbs sagged as Baba reached into her skirt pocket and brought out a handful of red, egg-shaped berries. Polly recognized them instantly as twisted stalk, a plant that tasted like cucumbers and grew by the river in the woods.

"This'll mask the taste of the valerian," Baba said. "Which, believe me, needs to be masked."

She squeezed the berries in her palm and drizzled the juice into the pot, then she lifted the plastic wrap off the neighbors' dishes. She ladled a spoonful of potion into each casserole.

"It's not Bree I'm worried about," Baba said with a sad smile. "It's your mom who'll need help making it through."

❧ ❧ ❧ ❧

After Baba left, a second round of visitors arrived. Friends who hadn't gotten the news until after work; reporters; even Miss Galloway, the young, melodramatic counselor at Laramie Junior High, who wanted to know if she could help. Polly went upstairs when they started organizing search parties. They were going to search the woods, but the way they talked, the way Miss Galloway's eyes got all watery, it was obvious they believed they were going in for a body.

Miss Galloway's job, as far as Polly could tell, was to give assemblies on worst-case scenarios. Laramie had a safe-school curriculum, which meant every kid had to know about things like longtime neighbors turning out to be child molesters and unpopular boys taking revenge with machine guns. They were in junior high now, Miss Galloway was always saying. It was time they grew up and Faced Facts.

The energy around Miss Galloway was lethargic and gray, hanging around her shoulders like a heavy, wet shawl. Focusing on those kinds of facts would sap the color from anyone. Abductions, torture, rape, murder, poverty, war, terrorism, AIDS, flu pandemics, hurricanes, tsunamis, global warming, everything you never wanted to know. Polly wanted to be the first person to *never* Face Facts. Let the police and Miss Galloway think the worst about Bree; this was the first time in months that Polly had had any hope for her sister.

Polly picked up her phone to call her best friend, Olivia.

They had each gotten private phone lines last Christmas, and neither of them was surprised when they tried to call each other at the same moment and got busy signals. They were always doing stuff like that, suddenly singing the same song or discovering that they'd eaten the same cereal for breakfast. Olivia lived on the outskirts of junior high society too. She was still baby-faced, dutiful, and something of a crier. Whenever she burst into tears over a B, she got teased.

Polly smiled when Olivia's line was busy, certain that Olivia was trying to call her at the same time. She hung up and waited for the phone to ring, but after a minute of silence, she dialed again. After three tries and nothing but busy signals, Polly began to feel uneasy. If Olivia wasn't calling Polly, whom was she talking to? She must have heard about Bree by now.

Just then, the phone rang. "Oh, Polly," Olivia said. "I just heard."

Polly felt such relief at the sound of Olivia's voice, she let out a weird sound.

"It's gonna be okay," Olivia said. "It will. You'll see."

Polly's eyes were dry, but her body was trembling. It didn't matter how awful Bree had been; once she was gone, it was a whole lot easier to love her.

"There's no sign of her yet?" Olivia asked softly.

"No. That's because she's in the woods."

"No way. Really? On her own?"

Polly realized it wasn't only sorrow that was making her shaky, but envy. Those were *her* woods. *She* should have been the one to go. "Yeah."

Olivia didn't scoff like everyone else, but she hesitated. "Are you sure? Do the police know?"

"They're starting a search, but they think it's for a body."

"Oh, Polly."

"They don't know the woods like I do. Meet me at Miller's Pond in an hour. I know we can find her."

"Now?" Olivia said. "My mom's making dinner, and it'll be dark soon. How about tomorrow? It's Saturday, so we'd have all day."

Polly couldn't believe what she was hearing. "Olivia, my sister's missing. Your mom will let you go. She always—"

"I better tell you," Olivia cut in. "I just got off the phone with Carly Leyland. She needs help on her algebra. You know how she's never talked to me before, but this time . . . she invited me over tonight. For a sleepover."

Polly felt like she'd been punched. Olivia wouldn't have a sleepover while Polly's family was falling apart, and even if she did, it wouldn't be with Carly Leyland. Olivia knew how Carly's father, Dan Leyland, had already bought up all the land around Baba's cottage and filled it with tract homes. Olivia had seen the same newscast Polly had—Dan Leyland touting his next plan for a massive mountaintop subdivision while Carly and her mother beamed in the background.

"I know what you're thinking," Olivia said, but Polly was pretty sure she had no idea. Olivia didn't know words like that.

"She was concerned about Bree," Olivia went on feebly.

"Yeah, right."

"Polly—"

"They're going to live in Mountain Winds themselves," Polly cut in. "You know where? In the only place my grandmother has ever found pyrola. Susie Lucas wouldn't be alive today if it wasn't for that plant. Nothing else would stop the bleeding after she had her baby."

"Look, just because her dad—"

"I thought you cared about the woods too," Polly said.

Olivia said nothing. Polly's father's voice echoed through the house, talking about search parties, flashlights, dogs.

"Great," Polly said. "Fine. My sister's missing and you've got Carly Leyland for your new best friend."

"Tomorrow, Polly," Olivia offered lamely.

"Bree could be dead tomorrow," Polly said, and hung up.

When the phone rang again, Polly yanked the cord from the wall. She stomped downstairs and through a room full of strange, pitying faces. Her mom sat hunched over on a stool in the kitchen, her eyelids sinking to half-mast; Baba's brew was obviously kicking in. Her mom's hand was on the phone, as if willing it to ring. When it remained silent, Polly knew she had to face one fact, at least: there comes a time when your mom can't make everything right again, when you have as much if not more power than she does.

Her mom made that moan again. The glow around her was thin and wavery, like a candle flame in the wind.

"That's it," Polly said. "I'm going to Baba's. I'm going to find Bree."

5

DEVIL'S CLUB
(Oplopanax horridus)

Devil's club gets its name from its sharp yellow spines. If left alone, it will quickly form a barbed wire–like fence, sometimes growing to twenty feet in height. The very young shoots are edible if the spines are not too sharp. An essential medicinal plant, devil's club is most often used for the treatment of infections, including tuberculosis.

$\mathcal{P}$olly raced past the throng in the living room and out into the yard. A crowd had gathered in the pink evening light, but when someone called her name, she didn't pause.

The road to her grandmother's house snaked through three sprawling subdivisions, but Polly knew a better route—a narrow badger trail through the woods behind her house. She ran across the lawn and easily leaped Sheep Creek. Breathing in the scent of river, moss, and pine, she immediately felt safer. The trees closed in around her, like a gaggle of protective friends.

There was just enough daylight left to search for cigarette butts and Bree's favorite diet-soda cans. For once, Polly prayed for litter, but all she found were survey stakes with pink ribbons and beetle-ravaged pines marked for removal. Unfortunately, logging in the area was nothing new. Polly's own grandfather had clear-cut this land forty years ago and might have harvested the second-growth pines as well if Polly's grandmother hadn't come along. Some said Baba bewitched him. In any case, soon after the wedding, Polly's grandfather nearly ruined this town by laying off half its work force and left the forest to its natural cycles of growth and disease.

People branded Baba as the villain, but now saw Carly Leyland's father, the owner of Leyland Corporation, as the hero riding in to save the day. Hiring hundreds of local men for his construction crews, Dan Leyland bought up the forest parcel by parcel and vowed to make the whole place habitable, pretty, and safe again, while adding a thousand homes to the ridges and valleys.

Polly felt like the only person, besides Baba, who liked the forest as it was—spooky, strange, and even ugly, like an old, gnarled woman with a tale to tell. She hated the wall Dan Leyland had put up, a six-foot-tall concrete monster between his precious subdivisions and the hazards of the wild.

Luckily, she knew where there was a gap. Polly rushed down the path and smiled when the wall stopped abruptly at her grandmother's yard, then started up again on the other side. A purple ash towered over Baba's garden—heaps of stinging nettle, mullein, and clover, pineapple weed, dandelion, and plantain, the plants most people in town yanked out by the roots.

Baba's humble wood cottage looked even more primitive surrounded by modern vinyl-sided tract homes. Baba had no lawn, while the new houses around her sported identical blue fescue. The only blue in Baba's yard was the turquoise fence she'd erected around her most potent herbs, such as pasqueflower, which slows the heart, and the beautiful pink-flowered jimsonweed, from the nightshade family, which Baba used to treat motion sickness.

As the last of the daylight faded a dog across the street lunged against his chain and barked. Polly could just make him out, a miserable creature tied to one of Leyland Corporation's signature cherry trees. Polly stepped up to the creaky blue gate, where Baba had installed a sign: WARNING! POTENT PLANTS AHEAD. ENTER AT YOUR OWN RISK.

Polly opened the gate, although it did seem risky. The garden released such a riot of scents, she felt dizzy. Baba had once said that half of a plant's potency comes from what a person believes it will do. Polly imagined spells rising from the plants and zipping past her, brushing her with luck and love and the ability to fly. By the time she reached the cottage, she was so unsteady she sat down on the porch.

The dog across the street barked once more then went quiet. Polly put her head down, then felt a cool finger on her neck.

"Does your mother know you're here?"

Her grandmother stepped out of a cottage that looked more like something sprouting from the earth than a house. It was hard for Polly to picture her mom growing up in a place where vines covered the windows, and sometimes Polly wondered if she really had. Maybe her mother had been adopted or suffered from amnesia. What else could explain why two people from the same family were so different? And why Polly's mom never came here anymore?

The dog suddenly threw back his head and howled. Baba walked straight to the shed, where she retrieved a menacing-looking tool with two curved, glistening blades.

"Steel cutters," she said, and walked across the street.

Polly glanced at the neighbor's dark windows before following her grandmother. The dog, a large husky, wore a torturous spiked chain around his neck and cowered as they approached. He had visible welts on his back, but what struck Polly more was the light around him, a silver glow rippling in the breeze.

"It's all right," Baba said. She touched the dog's head softly, and the light around him shimmered before he wagged his tail weakly. "You know your problem, Bronco? You keep coming back. Believe me, your owner doesn't deserve any more chances."

She glared at the house, then set her blade on the chain around the husky's neck, breaking it in one clean snap. As the horrible collar slipped away, Bronco shook his neck in relief and rolled over onto his back.

"No need for that," Baba said, but she rubbed his belly. "Best to run for the trees this time, Bronco. Head for the deep woods. That's what I'd do."

As if the dog understood her, he jumped to his feet and took off at a great gallop. Polly watched him until he disappeared in the woods.

"Aren't you afraid you'll get in trouble?" Polly asked.

Baba laughed. "Of course I'll get in trouble! Let me tell you something, Polly. If no one's upset with you, you're doing something wrong."

Polly's skin prickled. Whenever she was with her grandmother, stuff happened: dogs got away, people were healed, or Pastor Bentley showed up to try to cure Baba of her evil ways and her grandmother countered by offering him a glass of elderberry wine. Baba was blamed for everything that went wrong in their town, from the loss of all those logging jobs forty years ago to the local girls turning to Wicca. She was the common enemy, the one thing most people could all agree to hate.

And none of this bothered Baba one whit. She ignored the insults and went about her business. She knew just by looking at someone what hurt them and what they needed. She had a plant for every ailment, or so it seemed.

"What color am I today?" she asked suddenly, waving a hand above her head as if she could touch the light Polly saw.

Polly smiled. "Green," she said.

Her grandmother was always green. Green as the meadows, green as the woods. The color of compassion and strength.

Baba tilted her head, as if the answer surprised her. And just then Polly saw a flicker of orange in all that green. Then another of lavender. Beautiful colors, but Polly didn't like them. Her grandmother was *green*.

They crossed the street and put the steel cutters back in the shed.

"Now," Baba said, "I assume you're here for Bree."

❧ ❧ ❧ ❧

Polly imagined that after she found Bree huddling in some crude shelter in the forest, she would not only save her, she'd transform her. She'd wave her wand and make Bree someone everyone could love again. She'd give them all a second chance.

"Do you know where she is?" Polly asked her grandmother. The sky seemed to have drawn down closer, like a velvet scarf above their heads. Polly expected a quick, no-nonsense reply, but Baba stayed quiet.

"Baba?" Polly said. "Do you?"

Baba walked out of the yard and into the woods. She was getting older, but she still walked more in a day than most people walked in a month. She'd never owned a car and so she walked to the market for the few supplies she needed and through the woods, sometimes staying out all night. A few times she was gone for nearly a week, and the townspeople began to hope that she'd disappeared for good. Then she showed up in her garden again, a little dirtier maybe, but with her medicine bag full.

The woods behind Baba's house were relatively flat for fifty yards, then met the slope of Battlecreek Peak. Most people took the long five-mile trail around the mountain, but even in the growing darkness, Baba started straight up. Polly hurried after her, grabbing clump grasses and the trunks of white pines to keep her balance. By the time they reached the first forested summit, the velvet sky had become a vast black sea, and Baba was the only light around.

Baba leaned against a tree to catch her breath.

"Baba?" Polly said. "Are you all right?"

With every ragged breath, her grandmother's color changed —the green giving way to gold, then to red and blue.

"Listen," Baba said. "Can you hear that?"

Polly tilted her head. She heard chirping and gurgling and buzzing—the supposed silence of the forest.

"That's the sound of a million living creatures around you," Baba went on. "You're never alone, Polly. Don't think for a minute that you are."

They headed down another hill, then up again, past hundreds of trees tagged for logging. Only the light around Baba kept Polly from tripping over the survey stakes that stuck out of the ground like thorns. Polly felt a strange mix of horror and anticipation as they passed each marker; Baba wouldn't have come this way, where everything was going to change, unless she was leading Polly straight to her sister.

Finally, Baba slowed her pace, walking along a dangerous drop-off because there was a dense thicket of devil's club everywhere else. Baba used devil's club to treat lung ailments and bronchitis, though the plant looked more like a weapon than a cure. The shrub was eight feet high and armored, every foot-long leaf edged in spikes, each stem equipped with sharp yellow spines.

Yet her grandmother brushed her fingers along the serrated plant, and then suddenly dropped to her knees. In a flash she was gone, disappearing beneath the barbed-wire shrubbery through an opening Polly hadn't even noticed.

"Baba!" Polly shouted, but heard only silence. "Bree?"

The devil's club had its own aura, a dark green swirling mist. Polly crouched down and tried to follow her grandmother through the thin gap between plant and earth, but within seconds the leaves closed in around her. Something tugged at her scalp, and Polly realized her hair had snagged on the spiny leaves.

She tried not to panic. She wasn't trapped, she told herself; she'd crawled into a gleaming green cocoon. She couldn't move a hand to free her hair, so she took a chance and lunged forward, leaving a few curls like earrings on the lobes of the leaves.

Scalp stinging, she had just room enough to squirm forward on the ground, caterpillar-like. The tunnel seemed to go on forever, but eventually she saw light flickering between the leaves. A few more feet and she had to blink to adjust to the oddly bright sky.

At the end of the tunnel, Polly slowly got to her feet. In front of her stood her grandmother, surrounded by a grove of giant, glowing larches. Even without their auras, the larches were dazzling in their fall colors—every needle like a dagger of spun gold. The tree beside Baba was nearly 200 feet high, yet its most spectacular feature was what most people didn't see: a white, pulsing light around it in the shape of wings—thousands of them fluttering along the trunk and branches—as if the larch could lift off into the sky at any moment. There was no way Polly could have missed a dazzling spirit like that, yet she hadn't seen it from the other side of the devil's club.

"What is this place?" Polly asked. "Is Bree here?"

The grove was lit up like midday, and Polly could see every tree trunk; not a single one had been tagged. Baba looked delighted. The larches were her favorites—a feathery conifer that was green in spring, light and airy all summer, and blinding gold in fall. Unlike pines and firs, a larch changed color and dropped its needles every winter, revealing a tangle of bare black rigging that allowed the plants beneath it to thrive. Larches looked delicate, yet they grew at lightning speed, producing the strongest wood.

"I showed Bree this grove once," Baba said. "A long time ago."

Polly pretended to dust the dirt from her jeans, but she really wanted time to chase back the moisture in her eyes. She'd thought the woods were something only she and her grandma shared. She had never considered that Baba and Bree might have their secrets too.

Finally, she looked up. "I thought you were bringing me to her."

"Well," Baba said, "this would be a good place to stay, wouldn't it? The hares are always plentiful, the bearberries grow like mad, and water's not far away."

Baba gently tapped the trunk of the great tree. "You know why people say 'Knock on wood,' don't you?" she asked. "It's not superstition. It calls the spirit of the tree for help and guidance. Knock lightly and you won't be alone."

But Polly felt alone, even with Baba there. She might have hated her sister these last few months, but she still hadn't thought that Bree would leave her.

"This is where I first met your grandfather," Baba went on. "Forty-five years ago, he was out here cutting down every-thing in sight. He nearly took a saw to me, he was that intent on getting his lumber. Couldn't tell a woman from a tree! Imagine that."

She laughed, not like an old woman, but like a girl so beau-tiful and bewitching a man gave up his fortune to please her. Polly wished she'd met her grandfather and seen the way he looked at Baba, but he had died before she was born.

Baba wandered through the grove, lightly tapping every trunk, greeting each knot and branch as if they were old friends. But Polly felt exhausted now, disappointed even though the sight of the glowing larches was reason enough to have come.

"We'd better go," Polly said. "Mom'll be worried."

She turned to go and almost tripped over a ring of stones. Polly had been so dazzled by the trees, she'd missed the campfire still glowing and giving off heat. Her heart raced when she noticed a lock of charred blond hair on top of the red coals, as if the vainest girl in the world had cut it off for fuel.

Polly looked up at her grandmother, who stood by her favorite tree and smiled.

"Hmmm," Baba said.

6

BURDOCK

(*Arctium minus*)

Burdock abounds across North America, thanks to its hitchhiking Velcro-like seed burrs, which catch on clothes and animal fur. Rich in vitamins and iron, the whole plant, from roots to stems to leaves, is edible. The plant has been used as a powerful blood purifier for thousands of years, while its oils are a popular scalp treatment.

$\mathscr{P}$olly ran into the kitchen, where her mother still sat with her hand on the phone. She stood when she saw Polly's face, her legs a bit wobbly beneath her.

"You found her?"

Polly reached for the hair in her pocket and placed it on the table.

"No, but we found this."

Her mother stared at the charred strands. Baba's drugs must have been strong, because she didn't move.

"It's Bree's, Mom," Polly went on. "I know it is."

Her mom looked up, her eyes brimming with tears again. But it was fury that was causing them this time, not despair.

"Baba said that?" her mom asked.

"Well, not ex—"

"I can't believe this! I've never denied you time with your grandmother, Polly, but this is over the line. I won't have her raising false hopes. People *die* in the woods."

"You could have it checked," Polly said. "Like in *CSI*. Have the DNA tested."

Her mom swiped angrily at her tears. "Right now, it's all I can do just to survive this."

"Can't you at least tell the searchers we found it?" Polly asked. "It was in this amazing larch grove. The trees there are nearly two hundred feet high, but you don't see them. That's the weird thing. You've got to go through this thorny patch of devil's club, and there was this fire ring. It was still warm, Mom. Bree could have been there an hour before! After that I noticed the burdock roots someone had peeled the way Bree used to. Burdock's the only wild plant she ever liked."

Her mom turned away from Polly slowly. Her gaze fell on the lock of hair whether she wanted it to or not.

"Go on up now," her mother said. "I'll handle this."

※ ※ ※ ※

It was well after midnight when Polly's dad came in with the search party. Polly sprang out of bed but stopped halfway down the stairs at the sound of him weeping. The others in the group hurried their goodbyes and left.

". . . everywhere," he was saying. "Covered twenty square miles at least. No sign of her."

Except for the rare sound of his sobbing, it was silent. At last her mom said, "I know it's far-fetched, but Polly and my mother found this hair . . ."

Polly listened to her mother's almost embarrassed voice explaining about the fire and burdock roots. Polly's dad stopped crying. "That hair could belong to anyone, Faith," he said, his voice hoarse. "Even if it is Bree's, what does that prove? That she was in the woods once?" He paused, and Polly curled up on the step, her knees to her chest. "I'll talk to the police," he went on, "but I don't know if they'll test it."

Polly's mother was the one sobbing now. "Max Wendt told me if we don't find her within the first twenty-four hours, the chances that we ever will go way down," she said.

Polly ought to have been crying too, but the cold, ugly truth was that she wasn't sad. She was as different from her mom as her mom was from her grandma. Her mom couldn't imagine the best possibility and Polly refused to imagine the worst. She'd had her vision and she was sticking with it: like Bronco, the husky, Brianna Greene had gotten away.

The next morning, there were six policemen in the kitchen helping themselves to coffee. They stopped their talk of foul play when Polly entered the room.

"Where's my mom?" Polly asked.

As the men stared at their shoes, Polly heard voices in the yard. She hurried to the front door and found the lawn converted into an outdoor newsroom. Lights, reporters, and television cameras dotted the yard, and her mom and dad stood on a makeshift podium, arm in arm. Her mom was crying.

"If anyone has any information on our daughter," she spoke into the camera. "Anything. We just want her back. Bree? If you're out there, we just want you back."

A newsman kept snapping photos. *Click, click, click,* like a relentless woodpecker against the house. For the first time, Polly imagined what would happen if her sister didn't come back. At a certain point, they'd lock the door to Bree's room and no one would say her name anymore. Polly's mom's friends—the ones with children—would stop coming by, and Polly would no longer be Polly, but the sole child. The one who had to be so good and perfect that she made up for everything.

She tried to be quiet, but she must have made some sound because her dad left the podium. When his arms came around her, she pressed her face into his chest. All the girls at school wished they were older, but Polly wanted to go back in time. Back to when she was little, and her father could make everything right. But when her dad pulled back, his face straining to stay calm, she knew it was her turn to make things right for him. What he needed was a grownup—one daughter he didn't have to worry about at all. And because Polly would have given him anything, she smiled and told him she was better now. She didn't cry one drop.

ℵ ℵ ℵ ℵ

Polly's dad didn't go home to his cabin. He set up his blankets on the couch, but mostly he prowled the streets or went door to door handing out flyers. They created the handout on the computer, using an old picture of Bree because she hadn't allowed anyone to photograph her in the last few months. In it, she was tan and smiling, still with some flesh on her cheeks. No one knew her weight now, so they guessed.

MISSING 9/28/07: GIRL, 16, 5'5". AROUND 100 POUNDS. SHOULDER-LENGTH BLOND HAIR. BLUE EYES. MIGHT BE WEARING A DARK BLUE JACKET. REWARD FOR ANY INFORMATION! CALL (208) 555-4301.

That first weekend, Polly's mom bombarded the police with calls. She wanted round-the-clock search parties and updates on every lead. When divers pulled nothing but a rusted Jeep from Miller's Pond, she stared blankly at the water as if it had denied her its secrets. When the police tried to take her home, she ignored them and sat on the sand. She refused to talk to anyone, and by morning, when Polly's dad retrieved her, she was pale and silent as a ghost.

On Monday, there was no mention of school or work, and on Tuesday it was the same. By Wednesday, the visitors had stopped coming. Neighbors had done what they could, and the news must have gotten out that it was beyond grim in the Greenes' house. Polly remembered someone saying that it took three days for a spirit to rise. In their case, it took three days to turn their house into a tomb. The blinds were drawn, no one spoke above a whisper, and people turned their heads when passing on the street. Polly spent most of her time in her room, thinking that if she stood at her window and looked really, really hard, she could see a red light flickering in the boughs of the trees, a fairy coming to rest in the branches. She wondered if anyone out there could hear her mother's horrible cries coming from Bree's room, the Crying Room as she called it now.

🦋 🦋 🦋 🦋

Wednesday night, Polly cracked a window in her bedroom and thought enviously of Bree breathing in all that fresh air. If Polly had been the one to run away, she'd have loaded up first with food and warm winter clothes. It was just like her sister to leave without figuring out how she'd survive, expecting Polly to swoop in and save her.

Polly walked into her sister's room and rummaged through the dresser, picking out socks, a turtleneck, and long johns. She'd just slipped Bree's mittens into her pocket when she heard voices downstairs.

"Polly?" her dad called up. "Olivia's here."

Polly leaned against the wall, weak with relief. She'd been waiting for Olivia to come to her senses about Carly and beg for forgiveness, but before Polly even had a chance to be gracious, she heard Olivia's voice followed by Carly Leyland's.

Polly reached out, knocking one of Bree's pictures from the wall. Kneeling to pick it up, she came face to face with a photo of the Fab Five grinning in front of Jenny Gardner's lakeside cabin. This was their Before shot. Before the drugs, before Aaron and Brad, before the lies.

As Polly hung the photo back on the wall, Carly laughed —actually *laughed* in Polly's living room while her sister was on a missing-persons list. They'd hated each other ever since Carly's father offered Baba an exorbitant price for her house, and Polly's grandmother told him that that kind of money was for people who didn't know how to be happy. Carly called Polly's grandmother a lunatic, a nut case, a tree-hugging, devil-worshiping hag.

"Don't stand too close to Polly," Carly liked to tell the other girls at school. "She's got her grandmother's fleas."

Now, Polly heard Carly's sticky-sweet voice downstairs, the one she used around adults. People over thirty loved her; she was so well dressed and polite. And her father did so much for the community, building affordable housing, setting aside land in his subdivisions for parks and libraries.

"Mr. Greene," Carly said, "I couldn't believe it when I heard. It must be awful for you. I really hope everything turns out all right."

Polly rolled her eyes. Carly just wanted to know when the search parties would be leaving the woods so her dad could fire up his bulldozers.

"I'd better go see what's keeping Polly," her dad said.

Polly got into Bree's bed. The sheets still smelled like her sister, kind of sickly but sweet. She heard her father in her room next door, then he tapped softly on Bree's door.

"Polly?" he said.

"Tell them to go away."

"But it's Olivia down there."

Polly shook her head even though he couldn't see her. That wasn't Olivia.

"Tell her to go," she said.

She sensed him hesitating, then heard his heavy footsteps on the stairs. Maybe she'd been wrong about him needing her to grow up and be strong for him, because he did the most remarkable thing. He went down there and lied for her. He protected her the way he would a baby and told them both that she was asleep.

❧ ❧ ❧ ❧

Polly had stopped setting her alarm for school, but on Thursday her mother came in at seven, dressed in her work clothes. She'd missed a button on her blouse.

"All right," her mom said. "Time for school."

Polly rubbed her eyes. She was still halfway in a dream where she and Bree were in the woods picking mushrooms. Polly had to constantly knock the poisonous ones out of her sister's hands and ask her how she could be so stupid.

"What? I thought . . ."

"I have to go into work for a few hours." Her mom twisted her hands. "There's no choice. And you need to go to school. You need some normalcy."

Polly could have told her there was nothing normal about junior high, but she was still groggy, and her mother's deadened eyes stopped her.

"What about Dad?" Polly asked.

"Your dad went home."

Disappointment hit Polly in the stomach. She hadn't said

anything, but she'd thought it: with Bree gone, maybe her dad would stay. It wasn't so improbable. The day her dad had moved out, he'd told Polly he would always love her mother, but people change, lives head in different directions. Sometimes love isn't enough, he'd said, which to Polly seemed like the worst thing of all.

Still, if people could grow apart, then Polly thought they should also be able to grow back together. For the last week, her dad had made the coffee again and checked all the locks before going to bed. He had looked at her mother like he wanted her to ask him to stay; the problem was that her mother had never looked back.

Now, her mother sat on the edge of the bed, stiff and untouchable. She hadn't let anyone comfort her, not even Polly.

"I'm not ready," Polly said.

Her mother turned away. "Believe me," she said, "neither am I."

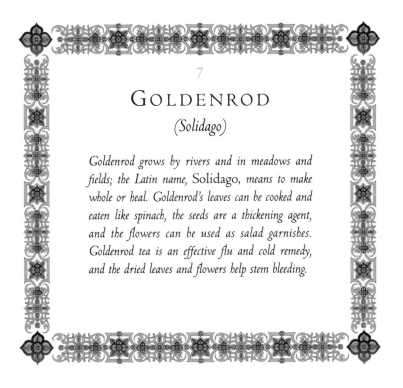

7

GOLDENROD
(*Solidago*)

*Goldenrod grows by rivers and in meadows and
fields; the Latin name,* Solidago, *means to make
whole or heal. Goldenrod's leaves can be cooked and
eaten like spinach, the seeds are a thickening agent,
and the flowers can be used as salad garnishes.
Goldenrod tea is an effective flu and cold remedy,
and the dried leaves and flowers help stem bleeding.*

$\mathcal{O}$n a good day, seventh grade at Laramie Junior High was
merely unpleasant. After Bree disappeared, it qualified as a
sick joke.

Kids Polly had known all her life gawked at her, while others whispered Bree's name along with words like *kidnapped* and
hacked up. Her first-period teacher cried whenever she looked
at Polly and ended class early just to wrap her in a hug.

"Oh, you poor, poor thing," Mrs. Ivie said as Mason

Halberton, one of Polly's classmates, walked by pretending to play a violin.

Polly tried to make a dash for it, but the principal was waiting in the hall with his condolences, along with the school secretary, who said she prayed for Polly's sister every night. Then Mandy Aloman and Bridget Stork showed up.

"Oh my God," Mandy said between bites of her Mars Bar. "Everybody's talking about it."

"Everyone needs to get a grip," Bridget said. "I'm *sure* she'll be back."

"Unless she was crushed by one of the giant troll people," Mason Halberton cut in. He had appeared behind them and hopped around as if he couldn't see past Mandy's backside. "Move it, troll."

Mandy's cheeks reddened, and Bridget whirled around. "What are you?" she said to Mason. "Blind, deaf, *and* dumb?"

Mason shrugged. "Yeah, well, at least I'm not a freak of nature. All brains and no beauty."

He plugged his nose, but when Bridget stepped toward him, he took off running down the hall.

"Idiot," Bridget said.

The girls walked together to debate class, but Polly held back at the door. She still hadn't worked out what she wanted to say to Olivia, but she needn't have worried. Her former best friend didn't even look at her. Olivia had moved her desk beside Carly Leyland's, and, worse than that, she'd cut her long brown hair into an exact replica of Carly's stylish chin-length bob.

Carly smiled like the cat who'd swallowed the canary. She leaned over to Olivia and said something that made the traitor laugh while Polly stumbled to her seat.

Mrs. Finch wrote the topic of the day's debate on the board, but Polly had trouble making sense of it. The floor was newly mopped, and more A papers had been pinned to the wall. She wanted to silence the students noisily taking out sheets of paper, but it appeared that no one had skipped a beat since she'd been gone. The PA speaker crackled to life, and Miss Galloway's disembodied voice burst into the room announcing an outdoor assembly. Mrs. Finch sighed and told them to follow her onto the soccer field.

Miss Galloway was already there, encouraging everyone to form a circle and hold hands. She was twenty-eight, Miss Galloway, a lover of wooden-bead necklaces and ponchos, rumored to be from Southern California.

Only the cheerleaders held hands. "Well, let's just be still then," Miss Galloway said. "I thought it only fitting that we take a moment to join in a prayer for Polly Greene's sister, Brianna. I'm sure you've all heard about the tragedy of her disappearance."

There were more stares and whispers, and Polly studied the ground. Someone giggled, and Miss Galloway glared in Carly Leyland's direction. Polly was surprised to see Joe

Meyer, Carly's boyfriend, telling Carly to be quiet. He glanced at Polly apologetically before Carly grabbed his arm and turned him around. Joe was Brad Meyer's younger brother, "an annoying little tattletale," according to Bree. She used to complain about the scenes Joe would make whenever he caught them doing drugs. "You'd think it was the end of the world!" Bree had once said.

Miss Galloway moved to the center of the circle. "Let's bow our heads now and offer a silent prayer for Brianna's safe return."

The silence became a rumble as people tried to get a good look at Polly. She felt like a whale that had washed up on the beach—a horrifying sight, but something everyone had to see, just the same. Embarrassingly, her legs began to tremble, and when she tried to still them, an elbow twitched. By the time Miss Galloway suggested a song, Polly's whole body had the tremors. It was almost a relief when Carly Leyland laughed again, because when everybody's gaze turned, Polly bolted.

Miss Galloway tried to call her back, but Polly was already into the thicket of raspberry bushes that lined the tiny creek behind the school. For a whole eight feet, it was like a mini-wilderness, thorny but green, and then the concrete began. The stream had never been more than a six-inch trickle, but when the Wal-Mart went in behind it, it was lined with cement to keep it in check. Miss Galloway found her by the stream later.

"When Bree comes back I'm going to kill her," Polly said.

The counselor put a hand on Polly's shoulder and led her back to class.

❧ ❧ ❧ ❧

Things didn't get much better when school let out. Polly used to meet Olivia by the water fountain, but today she put on her backpack and headed out the back door alone.

When she reached the forest's edge, she dashed into the woods as if it were her grandmother's arms. It was October, but the sun was warm and the scent of pines still thick in the air. Polly set out through a tangle of huckleberry bushes, their leaves already a glorious crimson. Huckleberries were always the first to change color, sometimes starting as early as July. Farther ahead, a meadow of goldenrod still bloomed. Polly picked a leaf and touched it to her tongue.

"Ugh," she said, puckering. Plenty of plants were edible, but Polly had found very few that tasted good. Still, according to Baba, goldenrod leaves could be added to soups and had been used by soldiers in the Crusades to stop bleeding on the battlefield. If Bree was in a fight for survival, she'd need a plant whose name meant "to heal."

Polly stuffed her backpack with leaves, then looked up to see her grandmother stepping out of the deep woods.

"Baba?" she said.

Her grandmother glanced behind her, and Polly quickly followed her gaze, wondering if she'd see a flash of blond hair or a blue winter coat.

"What are you doing out here?" Polly asked.

Baba stepped forward, tapping her medicine bag. "Gathering supplies, of course. And you?"

Polly looked up the mountain to get her bearings. Her mom always worried that she'd lose her way in the woods, but even in an unfamiliar part of the forest, Polly never panicked. Rivers lead to civilization, and trees lead away. Baba had taught her that.

"I'm going back to that grove you showed me," Polly said. "I've got some of Bree's clothes in my backpack, and I'm going to leave her the goldenrod, too."

Baba stared at her a long time, then at last she smiled. "Good," she said. She touched Polly's cheek and headed back toward her cottage, singing her favorite song, a poem she had set to music years ago.

Honey, child, honey, child, whither are you going?
Would you cast your jewels all to the breezes blowing?
Would you leave the mother who on golden grain has fed you?
Would you grieve the lover who is riding forth to wed you?

Mother mine, to the wild forest I am going,
Where upon the champa boughs the champa buds are blowing;
To the koil-haunted river-isles where lotus lilies glisten,
The voices of the fairy folk are calling me: O listen!

Polly listened until she couldn't hear anymore, then looked toward the woods again, the hairs on the back of her neck standing on end.

❦ ❦ ❦ ❦

Polly chose the sheer face of Battlecreek Peak as her marker and kept it on her right as she climbed. She retraced Baba's path to that magical grove, stopping twice to make sure she was going the right way. She sprinted when she finally saw the wall of devil's club.

This time she rose on tiptoes to try to see beyond the eight-foot-high shrub, but there was nothing there but the green tops of pine and fir trees—not a single golden-needled larch in sight. Someone else might have tried to solve the mystery, but Polly merely savored her goose bumps, certain that this place would be just as magical as she allowed it to be.

She walked the length of the devil's club, searching for the opening in the thorny wall. The shrub seemed thicker and pricklier than it had been when Baba was here, as if the tunnel had sealed itself up. Polly made a second pass, and a third, but the harder she looked, the thicker the devil's club seemed to be. Finally, she stepped back, glaring at the green light that bristled around the plant like a beast's spiky fur.

Then she saw where that fur parted, and a few pinpricks of white poked through. Polly quickly dropped to her belly and slithered into the small, thorny opening. It had grown thicker than last time, tearing up her arms and legs. She endured the cuts, along with a few more lost curls, and crawled to the end of the tunnel. The larch grove was there just as before, resplendent in gold, with light pulsing around every branch and needle. She hadn't noticed it with Baba, but even the air in the grove was different. Charged. It smelled of fire, but also of honeysuckle, a plant that Polly knew for a fact hadn't bloomed since July.

The fire pit had more charred blond hair inside it, along with two moldy, wet logs that had only smoldered.

"Bree?" Polly said.

There was no answer, not a breath of wind through the silken boughs of the larches. But Polly didn't feel alone. She removed her backpack, carefully taking out the goldenrod leaves along with the mittens and long johns and the blue turtleneck she'd picked out of Bree's dresser, and left everything on a boulder beside the fire pit.

"These are for you, Bree," she said. "Okay?"

Though she got no answer, Polly felt satisfied. She turned her attention to the moldy logs and decided that Bree needed tinder and dry branches. Searching the grove for the right wood, Polly built a fire house inside the pit the way Baba had taught her—the needles and bark first, like a floor; medium branches for the walls; and a solid, dry log for the roof.

All Bree would need was a spark. Something had burned here recently, but it was hard to picture Bree starting a blaze. Despite Baba's lessons on how to start a campfire with nothing but sticks and a shoelace and a bow-and-drill technique, Polly had never been able to produce more than a whiff of smoke, and Bree had called the whole thing stupid and struck a match. Reluctantly, Polly reached into her pocket and slipped out the book of matches she'd brought from home. Maybe this time Bree had waved a wand to spark a blaze, but Polly couldn't take any chances.

She thought about sparking up a campfire now, but before she could strike a match, she heard howling on the other side of the devil's club. She froze, her heart racing, as something or someone thrashed around. Polly was less afraid of bears or wolves than she was of some person discovering where Bree was hiding. Of course she wanted her sister to be found, but now that Polly had seen this grove, now that she'd felt the magic here, she thought that maybe Bree didn't want to be found *just yet.*

The howling came again. "Get off, you dumb plant! Get off!"

Polly straightened. That was no monster, or, if it was, it

was a familiar one. She crawled back into the tunnel and poked her head out the other side to find Olivia struggling against a giant spiny leaf that had attached itself to her arm.

Olivia, with her sporty new haircut. Olivia, the traitor.

❦ ❦ ❦ ❦

Olivia didn't notice Polly creeping out of the tunnel and covering up the entrance in the devil's club. In another life, Polly would have shown Olivia the grove and made it their own special hideaway, but not anymore.

"What are you doing here?" Polly asked.

Olivia jumped, and the giant leaf tore loose from her arm, taking some flesh and a few drops of blood with it. Olivia's eyes welled up with tears.

"Oh!" she said. "That thing is vicious."

Polly tried not to smile. At least the plants were on her side.

"I waited for you after school," Olivia went on, checking the rest of her body for damage.

"I wasn't going home."

"No kidding. I could hardly keep up with you." Olivia rubbed her arms and looked at Polly through her tears. "I know you're mad."

Polly scoffed. "You don't know anything."

"I know I should have been there for you. That first day. I'm sorry, Polly."

When Polly didn't respond, Olivia continued. "I know how you feel about Carly, but maybe you two could talk. You know, work things out?"

Polly squared her shoulders. "There's nothing to work out. Carly's evil."

Olivia shook her head. "She's not, Polly. She's just on a different side. I mean, her dad *is* trying to clean up the woods. Make it healthier, prettier. You could still—"

The look in Polly's eyes stopped her. "I could still what?" Polly asked. "Walk on a paved road between their perfectly trimmed pines? Swim in Carly Leyland's new swimming pool instead of Sheep Creek? You really think it's right to put houses up here? To tear out the trees and blow up wolf dens so people can have a better view? Why don't you just put in a shopping mall?"

Olivia would no longer meet her gaze. "It's not like that. I mean, when I talked to Carly, she made sense too."

Polly shook her head. Ever since they'd met, in first grade, Olivia had let Polly decide everything, from which movie they'd watch to what game they'd play. She'd always seemed content to follow Polly's lead, and though that had pleased Polly before, now it seemed like the scariest thing in the world—a friend who could be so easily swayed.

"You know what?" Polly said. "Go ahead and take her side. Maybe her dad will let you ride the bulldozer when they take down the first trees."

"Polly—"

"And you can tell Carly this isn't over. The woods don't belong to them. I don't care what papers they signed. And as long as Bree is out here, they can't do anything."

Polly expected Olivia to cry, but instead she reached for Polly's arm. It could have been the iciness of her fingers, but all the electricity and magic Polly had felt in the grove suddenly vanished.

"That's why I wanted to find you," Olivia said. "There are rumors, Polly. People are saying Bree isn't in the woods."

"Oh no? Then where is she?"

Olivia squeezed her tighter. "In another town, trying to figure out what to do. Polly, people are saying she left because she was pregnant."

Polly could only stare at her. "No," she said at last.

"Carly heard it from Joe. You know how his brother and your sister . . . Well, everyone knows how they were. It's not so hard to believe."

"Carly's lying," Polly said.

"Look, I just thought you should know. I thought—"

"Don't think anymore, okay? Just . . . don't."

Olivia looked close to crying again, but instead she turned and retreated down the mountain. Polly watched her go, thinking, *It's a lie. Carly always lies.*

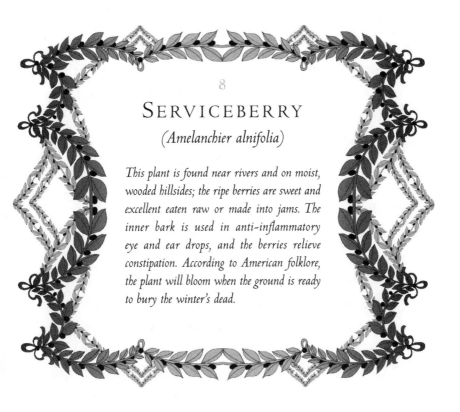

SERVICEBERRY
(Amelanchier alnifolia)

This plant is found near rivers and on moist, wooded hillsides; the ripe berries are sweet and excellent eaten raw or made into jams. The inner bark is used in anti-inflammatory eye and ear drops, and the berries relieve constipation. According to American folklore, the plant will bloom when the ground is ready to bury the winter's dead.

"*I* found more hair," Polly said.

Polly sat at the kitchen table while her mom put out cereal for dinner. Her mother was still in her work clothes; she'd had no choice but to go back to the office full-time. There were bills to pay, and it had been ten days now. Some people had already stopped asking about Bree first thing.

Polly had never thought much about her mom's job. It had been nothing but a bunch of big words—*ecosystem management, environmental regulatory compliance*—until her mom came home one day with a fat report labeled "Environmental Impact Analysis: Mountain Winds Development." Then everything made sense. Her mother was the one who had to decide when, or if, the Leyland Corporation could break ground in the woods.

"Please," her mom said, massaging her forehead. "You have to stop."

"But it's proof."

Her mom slammed her hand down on the table. "The police won't even test that lock of hair you gave me! What good would it do them? They say Bree could have been in the woods anytime, and they combed the forest. I've been out there too, Polly. What do you think I do during my lunch hour and after work?" Her eyes got all buggy, and Polly leaned away. "I go out there and leave things for her! Food, clothes, her winter boots. If there's even a chance that you were right . . ."

Polly nearly told her mom to ask Baba what she knew about Bree, but all of a sudden she wasn't sure if either of them really wanted to know the truth. If Baba wasn't watching over Bree, then what chance did her sister have to survive?

"I want you to come straight home from school every day," her mom said. "I can't worry about you too."

Polly stared into her bowl of bran flakes. *Why not?* she almost said. *Don't I count?* But by then her mom had gone up to the Crying Room, and conversation was done.

❦ ❦ ❦ ❦

Jenny Gardner and Kate Eardly, two members of Bree's Fab Five, showed up Tuesday after school. Polly opened the door and got a scare, as she always did, at the sight of their black-rimmed eyes and pale faces. They used to be pretty, but now they were ghouls dressed in black boots, white makeup, and AC/DC T-shirts. Polly couldn't even tell the color of their auras, yet they were smiling, something they'd rarely done before.

"Polly," Jenny said. "You mind if we come in a minute?"

Polly did mind, actually. Her mother was at work and her dad a half-hour drive away. What if one of the Fab Five took out a knife? She had no idea what they were capable of.

"Um."

"Look," Kate said, "we know it's, like, not exactly Disneyland at your house these days, but we left some things in Bree's room."

They slipped into the living room like shadows. Jenny walked to the fireplace, where she smirked at an outdated family photo—Polly's mom and dad with their arms around each other, Bree and Polly pigtailed and smiling in front. Jenny had vampire eyes, so light green they were almost clear.

"My mom will be home soon," Polly said, hoping that would make them leave.

"We'll just be a second," Jenny promised.

They headed upstairs, and though Polly knew she ought to stop them, she wasn't sure how. In the past, they'd always played deaf when she spoke to them, or pretended they couldn't see her. She followed them into the Crying Room, where they began pawing through Bree's dresser drawers.

Polly knew what they were looking for: pot, cocaine, the latest pills. Jenny went to the closet and grabbed Bree's suede jacket. After rummaging through the pockets, she tossed the coat on the floor and yanked at a blouse.

"Hey!" Polly said.

Neither of them listened. Kate spilled out the contents of jewelry boxes while Jenny overturned the desk drawer. Polly could have told them that the police had already gone through all of Bree's things and so had her mother and father, but her throat felt swollen shut.

They turned the room inside out, finding nothing, then Jenny stomped to the open window. When she reached into her pocket for a tightly rolled joint, Kate made a grunting noise, like an infant growing hungry in her sleep. Jenny lit the joint and inhaled deeply, then turned her eerie gaze on Polly.

"Want some?" she asked.

Polly had been moving away; now she froze. She was shocked, horrified, and strangely, terribly thrilled. How many times had she put her ear to the wall to try to hear them? How many times had she loitered outside Bree's room, hoping they'd ask her to come in, hang out? They were revolting and fascinating, everything she didn't want to be, yet so daring and indifferent she couldn't help but admire them. If Bree were here, she'd chase Polly out of the room and tell her to get her own life. But Bree was not here. The Fab Five hadn't even asked about her.

She glanced over her shoulder. Kate watched her with a smirk, as if this were everyday stuff. Another twelve-year-old converted. Polly would never be like Bree, but what harm could it do to take one puff? Just to see what all the fuss was about.

She watched the smoke rise like a genie out of a bottle and felt her heart hammering in her chest. But the moment she stepped forward, Jenny shrieked. A dragonfly had flown in the open window and buzzed past her lips.

"My God!" Jenny said, jumping away from the sill. "What is that thing?"

Kate put her hands over her head as the red-bellied creature whizzed toward her. Maybe it wasn't a dragonfly at all, but a colorful, shapely moth. As it circled Kate's head, Polly saw long, tattered wings and pinprick eyes of blue.

Polly stepped back, startled, as Jenny flailed her arms. The dragonfly—or whatever it was—pirouetted and flew out the window.

"Did you see that?" Jenny asked. "It looked almost like . . ."

She paused, and Polly held her breath, waiting for her to say it. Waiting for someone cold and cynical to admit that if awful, vile things happened in the world, then magical, wonderful things must happen too. But Jenny merely shook her head, as if shaking off the vision.

Polly hardly noticed when they left. She stood at the window and drank in the sight of the dragonfly doing loop-the-loops—a showoff if Polly ever saw one, tattered wings and all. Polly gripped the window ledge and thought of how close she'd come to ruining everything. It was too much to believe, which was exactly why she liked it. That was no insect but her sister, come to save *her*.

ꕙ ꕙ ꕙ ꕙ

Polly was taking an algebra quiz when the first bulldozer rumbled by.

"Dad got the go-ahead for Mountain Winds," Carly announced to the class.

Polly stared at her test, but the numbers swam. Her mom must have handed over her environmental impact report, the one that said there was nothing in the woods worth protecting. Polly listened to the slow crawl of heavy equipment and stumbled through the remainder of the test. When the bell rang, she took one look toward her next class and headed the other way.

Racing out of school toward the forest, she hardly noticed the light sprinkle or the puddles in the streets. Still a quarter mile from the woods, she knew that everything had changed. There, on a giant billboard, the sign had already gone up.

MOUNTAIN WINDS—HEAVEN ON EARTH!
1,000 LUXURY-HOME SITES.
TAKING RESERVATIONS NOW!

On the edge of the woods, a double-wide trailer had been set up as a construction office, and a rough, new dirt road led into the trees. Polly bent forward, feeling dizzy. In the distance she heard diesel engines, chain saws, the rumbling of bulldozers. A tree shrieked as it fell and thudded against the earth.

With a lump in her throat, she followed the new road. For a few minutes, the forest looked safe and intact, and she dared to think that everything would be all right. Then she rounded a turn and met a traffic jam of construction equipment, men with chain saws, and downed trees. A man in the cab of one of the bulldozers gestured for her to go back, but when she just stood there he shrugged and lowered his blade. Polly watched, horrified, as he tore a lush thicket of serviceberries from the ground. She could have picked the dark purple berries and dried them for Bree to eat all winter. She could have simmered the inner bark to make a salve for sore eyes.

Her own eyes burned at her helplessness, and then, suddenly, the men stopped their engines. She couldn't understand what was happening until she realized she was soaked. The light mist had turned to a steady downpour and the men headed for shelter in the trailer.

Alone, Polly laid her head on a fallen white pine. It still had a dim green energy around it, but as she stood there, the color faded away. The few tears she shed got her nowhere. Hands in fists, she ignored the rain, along with the laughter of the men in the trailer, and walked out of the woods. The construction workers just wanted a paycheck. What she wanted was someone to blame.

🦋 🦋 🦋 🦋

In the rain, the squat gray office building looked even uglier than usual. Polly grabbed a rock from the stark landscaping bed of stunted pines and prickly junipers, and aimed for her mother's office on the second floor. She smiled grimly when she hit the metal trim with a satisfying *thwack,* and her mom's pale face appeared in the window. The enemy was in sight.

Her mom came out the door a moment later, pulling on her jacket. "What are you doing? Did something happen? Is it Bree?"

Polly didn't hesitate. "How could you give them the permits?" she shouted. "How could you let them build up there?"

Her mom had grabbed her wrist, but now she let go. "Is

that what this is about? You left school to talk about some lit-tle development?"

"It's not little!" Polly was screaming so loudly, two men on the second floor looked out. "Did you know they're tearing down the trees right now?"

Her mom narrowed her eyes. "Did you go up there? To the woods?"

"Yes. After I saw the equipment go by."

"I can't believe this," her mom said. "You just walked out of school and thought you'd go for a little hike? Do you re-alize you'll get a truancy?"

"You should have told me they were going to start build-ing!" Polly said.

"I should have done no such thing," her mom countered. "This is my job, Polly. I surveyed the soil and plants and wrote up my usual report. They have every right to build up there. There's nothing special about that land."

Polly felt like she'd been hit. As if another tree had come down, this time in her own yard. "Except that Bree's there," she said.

Her mother looked almost in pain. "Oh, Polly."

Polly widened her stance. "You must think she's there. You've been leaving things for her."

Her mother's eyes looked wild for a moment before she turned away. "I'd do anything if I thought there was a chance she'd . . . She's not taking them, Polly. The boots, the food. They're right where I left them."

Polly shook her head. Maybe Baba was bringing Bree food or, even better, Bree was learning to fend for herself. "She'll take them when she needs them," she said, "but not if you let them tear down the woods around her."

"I'm not letting anyone do anything. My office is in charge of the environmental impact study. That's all. I'm not going to have this conversation. You have to go back to school."

Polly didn't budge. She'd make her mother drive her back and shove her into class. Even Bree would be impressed with her lack of surrender.

"Don't take that tone with me," her mom said, even though Polly hadn't spoken a word. She almost looked behind her to see if Bree was there. She hadn't heard her mother sound so furious and fed up since before her sister disappeared.

"And don't ever throw a rock at my window again," her mom went on. "I was done with that the day I moved out of your grandmother's house."

Polly tried to hold on to her mutinous gaze, but her mom was shaking.

"It was Baba they were aiming for," Polly said, her bottom lip trembling, the cold starting to get to her, too. "People have always been out to get her."

"Yes, and I paid the price. You have no idea what I've had to do to make people treat us the same as everyone else."

"I know exactly what you did! You stopped loving Dad when he quit his job and got too weird for you. You cared more about what the neighbors thought than your own marriage."

"There was more to it than that, Polly."

"No there wasn't!" Polly said. "He still loves you. I know he does."

"Polly—"

"You pushed Bree away too! You didn't care about the drugs, you just couldn't stand to think that people would start talking about us again."

Her mom might have started crying, but in the rain it was hard to tell. And Polly was on a roll now.

"Well, guess what," Polly went on, hardly knowing where the words came from, hardly recognizing herself. "People are talking. You want to know what they're saying? They're saying Bree didn't run away because she was doped up. They're saying she ran away because she was pregnant."

Even in the rain, Polly could see the color drain from her mother's face. And all at once, Polly thought, *I'm sorry, I'm sorry, I'm sorry,* but she knew the words came too late.

"Mom, I'm s—"

"Don't even think about going back to the woods," her mom said. "Not today or any day. You're grounded. Get in the car."

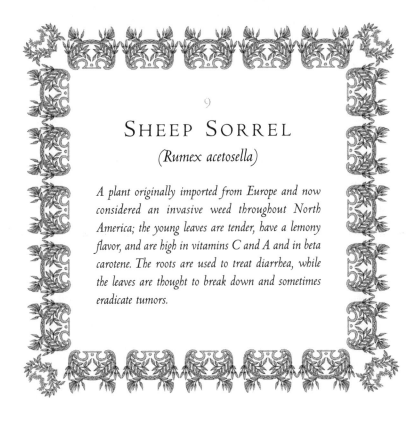

9

SHEEP SORREL

(Rumex acetosella)

A plant originally imported from Europe and now considered an invasive weed throughout North America; the young leaves are tender, have a lemony flavor, and are high in vitamins C and A and in beta carotene. The roots are used to treat diarrhea, while the leaves are thought to break down and sometimes eradicate tumors.

Every night, Polly dreamed she sprouted wings and flew away. In the dream, Baba brought her food and blankets, but unlike Bree, Polly didn't need them. She lived in the grove and survived on nothing but nectar and freedom. If it had been her, she'd have proved it could be done.

But when she woke, her powers vanished. Grounded for two weeks, Polly served time at her bedroom window, wondering how her sister was coping with the blustery weather, unable to do anything but watch the last of the leaves fall.

After school one afternoon, Polly whirled away from the window, as helpless as Tinker Bell trapped under glass. Her hair slapped her face as usual, and she tugged at an unruly curl. She'd always loved her grandmother's long, unbridled hair, the way it swirled in the wind like a wild creature itself, but what Polly needed was short hair that wouldn't get tangled in the thorns of the devil's club. What she needed was something to do.

So she grabbed a pair of scissors and, before she could lose her nerve, hacked off her curls above her ears. Then she opened the window and tossed the ringlets out, satisfied that at least a part of her would be out there where Bree was.

Later, she heard her mom come in from work and immediately pick up the phone. Her mother refused to talk about the possibility that Bree was pregnant, but every night she called more women's clinics and asked if anyone fitting Bree's description had come in. By the time Polly walked downstairs, her mom had closed the phone book and sat with her head in her hands.

Polly swung her head from side to side. She hadn't realized how much extra weight she'd been carrying around.

"Mom?"

Her mother raised her head and flinched. "Oh, Polly," she said. "What have you done?"

"I like it. It's a pixie cut."

"Are you crazy? We'll have to take you to the salon to get it fixed."

"No!" Polly said, stepping forward. "I told you I like it."

"How can you? It's uneven."

Polly shrugged. "So what?"

"*So what?*" Her mother got to her feet, looking confused and horrified, as if she were dealing with someone from another culture—someone who ate bugs or wore war paint to breakfast.

"I can't believe this," her mom said. "I can't believe you'd do this to me."

"This isn't about you!" Polly said. "It's got nothing to do with you at all."

"This is your grandmother's doing." Her mother grabbed her purse and headed toward the garage. "Come on. *Now.*"

They'd forgotten dinner, but that wasn't why Polly's stomach hurt. They didn't have to speak during the ten-minute drive to Baba's house to know what the other was thinking: *I don't like you anymore.*

❧ ❧ ❧ ❧

Baba's bonfire was visible from down the street, a six-foot-high blaze in the middle of her gravel driveway. It was the night of the full moon, which was when Baba always burned her garden debris and fed the ashes back into the soil. Polly was surprised that the neighbors weren't standing in their yards armed with garden hoses.

Polly's mom stopped the car beside the fire ring and got out. "Mom!" she shouted. "Do you see this? Do you see what you've done?"

Baba stepped around the flames in a long black skirt, a man's work shirt, and muddy hiking boots. Polly would have given anything to have a mother like her—a mother who thought the ugliest, dirtiest, weirdest things beautiful. Maybe her own mother knew this. Maybe that's what this was all about.

"What?" Baba said. "Turned Polly into a lovely young lady?"

Polly got out of the car beaming, but her mother started to cry. "She had beautiful hair. Like mine, only pretty."

A wolf howled in the distance while Baba checked that her fire was well contained. "Let's go inside," she said.

Baba's kitchen was more like an extension of her garden than a room, smelling of mint and sage and pine, every countertop and shelf piled with herbs. It looked chaotic, but Baba knew where everything was and picked a variety of leaves to make them all tea.

"I can't do it anymore," Polly's mom said.

"Don't be silly," Baba told her, clearing off roots and seeds to make room at the table. She set out three cups and poured boiling water over her tea leaves, then sweetened the brews with cream. "You *are* doing it. You get up every morning and breathe. That's all anyone's asking."

Polly's mom usually steered clear of Baba's teas, but this time she sat down and drank greedily, as if hoping for something to knock her out.

"Did I ever tell you," Baba said, easing herself into a chair and looking at Polly, "about the night someone tried to burn down this house?"

Polly loved her grandmother's stories, but tonight nothing could compete with the colors dancing around Baba's head. Arcs of red, orange, and purple—a rainbow she didn't dare look away from for fear that when she turned back it would be gone.

Baba winked. "It started with the rocks, as usual," she said. "They broke the living room window, then someone set a rag on fire and tossed it in. I came in to find my curtains going up in flames."

"Did the house burn down?" Polly asked, still gawking at that rainbow.

"Heavens, no. I put out the flames with a pitcher of water, though I did switch to blinds after that. That was the night your mother was born."

Polly's mom finally looked up. "You scare people, Mom."

Baba shrugged. "Only those who are already afraid."

"What have you ever done that was so awful?" Polly asked.

"You help people no one else will touch! The ones with nowhere else to turn."

Baba laughed. "Yes, but I have too much fun doing it, and to many people, life is serious business. And then there's the problem of me not caring what anybody thinks. Let me tell you, Polly, I've found indifference to be quite a powerful thing."

Polly knew her grandmother had spiked each tea differently when her mom's head began to bob.

"I think I need to lie down," her mother said.

Polly and Baba helped her to the couch. Polly's mom glared at Baba as her eyes began to close, but in seconds she was curled up, asleep.

"You drugged her," Polly said.

Her grandma smiled. "She needed to stay here tonight and rest. And I want to see what you've been up to at the grove."

"I'm grounded," Polly said. "I'm not supposed to go to the woods."

Baba looked at her sideways, as if to say that what you're supposed to do has nothing to do with anything. Polly couldn't believe how much she loved her.

"Let me put out the bonfire," Baba said, "and you'll lead the way."

Under the full moon, Polly could see everything from the dark green fuzz on the pine boughs to the startling gold of a screech owl's eyes. Her new haircut made her feel quick and nearly weightless. Fairylike, freed from glass, drawn toward the Dark Lands.

"You know there's an abandoned miners' cabin about a mile northwest of here," Baba said. "Nice and secluded, up the second gully past Willow Creek."

Polly glanced at her, her palms suddenly sweaty despite the chilly night. "Yeah?"

"Now, I wouldn't live in it. Too dreary and grim. I'd find myself a cave or build a lean-to. But some people might like it, especially when the snows get real deep. You need just three things to survive: water, food, and shelter. The rest is decoration."

Polly knew this was the moment to ask where Bree was. But suddenly it seemed like the truth always had some ugliness or disappointment in it. Either Baba didn't know where Bree was, or else she was willing to put Polly and her parents through hell to keep Bree safe. Polly didn't know which was worse.

Polly saw the last of the sheep sorrel in the moonlight and stooped to pick the leaves. She answered the unspoken question herself. "I'll take this to Bree in the grove."

Her grandmother nodded, and as Polly stood she saw all

those colors around Baba again, the rainbow. It wasn't the moon at all but her grandmother who lit up the mountain.

❧ ❧ ❧ ❧

When they paused to catch their breath, the forest did the same. The wind stopped rustling through the trees and the birds suddenly grew silent.

"I used to be able to look at a person and know what was wrong with them," Baba said. "But last week I mistook Julie Benson's gas bubble for a broken heart. Luckily, vervain works on both."

"You're an amazing healer, Baba," Polly said. "I can only see colors around people, and sometimes shapes. What good does that do?"

Baba laughed. "But that's everything! You see a person's true colors. You have no idea how powerful you are." She paused. "You see something around me?"

Polly shook her head. She would rather watch the whole forest come down than talk about that rainbow. It was mesmerizing, but also the last thing you saw after a storm. The last thing.

"Polly," Baba said, taking her chin in her hand. "You think anything you can say will scare me?"

Polly shook her head. "Nothing scares you."

Baba let go of her chin and laughed softly. "Oh, that's not

true. Your mother terrifies me. Going into botany, turning the magic of plants into science. Marrying a dull man, then divorcing him just when he got interesting. *That's* scary."

Though the harebells had faded, a blue glow still hovered where the flowers had been and ghostly green auras shot up where grass blades would come in spring.

"A rainbow," Polly said at last.

Baba nodded and touched Polly's shoulder. "Oh, I'd like to see that. I never saw color. Just secrets. Pain."

❦ ❦ ❦ ❦

Twenty minutes later, they arrived at the grove. All the needles on the larches had fallen, leaving the limbs as bare and smooth as bone. Between the full moon and the fluttering white light around the trees, the grove was as bright as day. Baba went to the oldest, tallest tree and pressed her cheek to the trunk.

"When I first came here," Baba said, "Edward's company never even thought about replanting the forests they cut. They thought the trees went on forever." She sighed, the last part of it turning to a cough. Polly shivered beneath jeans and a thick flannel shirt, and her grandmother hugged one of the larches for warmth.

"I tried to convince him to change his ways," Baba went on. "Tried to bring him out here under a full moon like this one and make him sit a spell, but he was so antsy! He could never stay still long enough to really see anything. They were just trees to him. Lumber. There was big money to be made. He loved me, but he was who he was."

"So what happened?" Polly asked.

Baba shrugged. "That's it."

"That's it?"

When her grandma nodded, Polly put a hand on her hip. "That's a really bad story, Baba."

Her grandmother laughed, her breath coming out in a thick puff of smoke. "Most happy endings are. They're dull as dishwater."

"But you didn't say how you changed his mind."

"I didn't. You can't change anyone's mind, Polly. But one day someone may love you enough to make a sacrifice."

Before Polly could respond, her grandmother bent over a tangle of fallen limbs and picked out a strong, thin piece of larch.

"This can be our bow," she said. "Find some poplar wood for a drill and fireboard and make me a fire, Polly."

Polly glanced toward the ring of stones where the fire house she'd built for Bree had been burned down to ashes and the matchbook still sat, unused, on a rock. How had Bree done it? Polly had tried the bow-and-drill technique a hundred times and had never been able to produce more than smoke.

Yet Baba was already off in search of tinder. Reluctantly, Polly gathered an armful of poplar wood, then found her grandmother removing a leather lace from her boot.

"You remember how to make fixed loops on the bow?" Baba asked.

Polly nodded and set down her wood. Her grandmother watched closely as she knotted the shoelace on either end of the larch branch, pulling it taut to make a curved bow.

"Good," Baba said. "What do you do next?"

Polly may have never sparked her own fire, but she still knew all the steps. First, she stacked dry wood and tinder in the fire pit, then she sorted through the soft poplar wood for a spindle and fireboard.

"Put a notch in the fireboard," Baba reminded her, "for the spindle to sit in."

As Baba hummed happily, Polly used a sharp piece of larch to make the notch. Kneeling on the fireboard, she looped the bow lace around the eight-inch-long spindle, then set one end of the spindle in the notch. Holding the other end steady with a rock, she began sawing the bow back and forth. The spindle turned, and eventually the friction was supposed to produce an ember she could transfer to the dry tinder and fan into a flame. When her grandmother did it, the whole process took ten minutes or less.

But after ten minutes, Polly's arm ached and the rock

slipped from her moist palm. She started again, only to have the spindle spin out, losing what little heat she'd mustered. Again, Polly repositioned her bow and started sawing. She kept up the motion for fifteen minutes, until the lace on the bow snapped.

Polly dropped the bow, trying not to cry. Her grandmother squeezed her shoulder.

"That's why we have two feet."

Baba removed the lace from the other boot and handed it to her. Fighting tears, Polly strung the bow once more and knelt back down on the cold ground. She had no idea how much time passed, though it felt like hours. She sawed without enthusiasm, without much hope of a spark at all.

When her motion slowed, her grandmother said, "We'll have to leave if we can't get a fire started soon."

"I'm doing my best!" Polly said. Just then the bow slipped from her fingers, and she flung it aside in frustration. "It's too hard! There's no way Bree could do this."

Her grandmother retrieved the bow but didn't hand it to her. "Well then," she said, "we might as well give up."

Polly got to her feet. "Yes, we should!"

There. She'd said it. She couldn't make fire from a couple of sticks, and she certainly couldn't make everything right. Baba watched her as she snatched the matchbook off the rocks and opened the flap. All the matches her sister hadn't used were in there. Someone had been out here starting fires, but at that moment, Polly couldn't believe it was Bree. She knew, deep down, how impossible Bree's survival was.

Polly tore a match from the book and struck it, holding the flame above the tinder. She was just about to drop it in when she felt the breeze on her back. The winged white auras around the larches had begun to flutter, and more than that, they were no longer white. Maybe the colors had always been there and she just hadn't noticed, but now each tree seemed to have its own personality—one cool blue, another sunny yellow, the showiest ones a glittering pink. It was as if the larches got up and danced when no one was looking and Baba smiled as if this was all perfectly ordinary—in her world, the impossible happened every day.

Polly rushed back to her grandmother, wanting the impossible more than she'd ever wanted anything else. She grabbed the bow and sawed furiously, not caring if she went too fast, not caring how irrational or dumb it was to believe that if she could make fire, then Bree could make it too.

After ten, fifteen, twenty minutes—she lost track of time—smoke wafted out between the spindle and fireboard. She would have stopped sawing, but her grandmother knelt beside her.

"This is the critical time," Baba said softly. "Increase your downward pressure a bit. That'll make a little dent in the fireboard, where the coal will start."

Polly wanted to check for the coal immediately but kept

sawing until her grandmother told her it was time. With trembling hands, she lifted the spindle, and there it was. A tiny ember, the littlest thing.

"Don't blow," Baba said. "That'll put it out. Just give it a little oxygen by waving your hand." Polly waved until the tiny coal began to glow. "That's it. Now move it carefully to the tinder."

Polly was so excited she nearly knocked the ember off the fireboard, but she managed to get it safely to the stack of tinder and tap it out. The coal slipped in among the twigs and needles, and went out.

"No!" Polly said. The tears started just as a whiff of smoke began to rise. She looked up through blurry eyes at her grandmother.

"Go on, now," Baba said. "Blow."

Polly blew on the tinder until, with a *whoosh*, the smoke ignited into flames.

"You see?" her grandmother said. "Everything's going to be fine."

Polly was surprised to find herself sobbing. She reached through both Baba's rainbow and the colors from the trees to hug her grandmother. "Don't die, Baba," she said. "I need you."

Her grandmother just held her as sparks from the fire burst toward the sky.

10

CREEPING DOGBANE

(*Apocynum androsaemifolium*)

The name dogbane *comes from the root's reputed value as a remedy for the bites of mad dogs. Though often poisonous as a food, dogbane is still used internally by Native Americans to treat everything from headaches to insanity to cancer. Warning! Dogbane should be used with great caution, and only under the care of a qualified practitioner. It can dramatically slow the pulse.*

 Polly and her grandmother didn't return to the cottage until morning.

"What did you put in my tea?" Polly's mom cried the moment they walked in. The tiredness in her eyes was gone, replaced by sparks of fury.

Baba tried to look offended, but she was battling a smile. "Just something soothing. You were so worked up."

"Worked up? Look at her!" Polly's mom swatted at Polly's hair, letting loose a shower of dirt and needles. Polly's sneakers were caked with mud, her jeans torn and dirty, her flannel shirt more brown than red. But none of that mattered to Polly because last night, she'd kept her fire burning. Baba had sat beside the flames, as contented as a cat.

"You took Polly to the woods, didn't you?" her mom went on. "Where I've forbidden her to go. Didn't you hear the wolves? Did you consider for one minute that you were putting the only child I've got left in danger?"

Baba's face fell as a double rainbow took shape around her. "I suppose I didn't," her grandmother said quietly.

Even Polly's mother seemed surprised at this rare capitulation. She opened her mouth, then closed it. "Well," she said. "We're late. You've got school, Polly, if you haven't forgotten, and I've got a meeting at work. I won't even have time to change."

Baba eased herself down on the couch, her eyes dull with pain.

"Are you all right, Baba?" Polly asked.

Her grandma smiled weakly. "Go on. I'll be fine."

The light around Baba's lips turned pink, a color Polly often saw around people in love and, ironically, also around those who lied. Her grandmother's hands trembled and in the full light of day looked as crinkly and brittle as autumn leaves. Polly would have refused to leave her, except that she remembered what Baba always said: when there's a problem, girls, run for the trees. There had to be something in the woods that would save her grandmother—maybe an herb so powerful even Baba had never dared to use it before.

Polly hugged Baba tightly, then followed her mother to the car.

"You can't go to school like that," her mom said as she backed out of the driveway. "I'll take you home to shower. You'll be late, but I'll write you a note."

"No," Polly said, shaking pine needles from her hair. "I'm going like this."

"Don't be ridiculous, Polly."

"I'm not! I don't care what the kids say. It's nothing I haven't heard before."

They were two blocks from home, and Polly felt strangely calm. She'd search the woods for a cure for Baba, leave roots and berries for Bree, even go to school covered in mud. The key, she thought, was just to do *something*, even if people thought the things she did were dumb.

Her mother turned down their street and pulled into the driveway, but she didn't turn off the car. Neither of them moved.

"What do the kids say about you?" her mom asked.

Polly turned away. This was the last thing she wanted to talk about. She didn't fit in, but so what? Neither did Baba. It didn't matter; Polly told herself that a dozen times a day.

Baba had gone her whole life as an outcast, a misfit, and was probably the happiest person in town.

But for all Polly's mom knew, Polly was the most popular kid in seventh grade. Popularity mattered to Faith Greene. She might have hated Bree's friends, but Polly could tell she was relieved that she had some.

"Nothing. You know. The usual stuff," Polly muttered.

Her mom stared at her, then surprised her by putting the car in reverse. They skidded back up the driveway, her mom gripping the wheel.

"Mom?"

Her mom didn't say a word as they drove to Laramie Junior High and into the ten-second-drop-off lane. As usual, Mr. Blakely, the principal, was standing on the curb, motioning for parents to keep their minivans moving. Mr. Blakely was a former high-ranking military man who now carried a stopwatch around a Podunk junior high. For some reason, it made him furious when people couldn't say goodbye in ten seconds or less.

Polly put her hand on the door as they neared the drop-off point, but when her mom pulled into position, she said, "Wait."

Polly couldn't believe it when her mom turned off the engine. With a dozen cars lined up behind them and Mr. Blakely already sprinting forward, her mom took her hands off the wheel. To most people, it would have been a silly little act of defiance, yet Polly knew it was the single bravest thing her mother had done.

Mr. Blakely rapped on the window just as Polly's mom opened her arms. Polly shot across the seat and into her mother's embrace.

"I was the witch's daughter," her mom said, burying her nose in Polly's choppy, dirty hair. "When your grandmother walked me to school, she was always in some outlandish outfit, oblivious to the things people said about her, or me."

Polly didn't speak for fear her mother would pull away.

"You're *fine* the way you are," her mom went on vehemently. "You hear me?"

Principal Blakely held up his stopwatch and Polly's mom laughed nervously.

"One Mississippi," her mother said. "Two Mississippi, three Mississippi . . ." Her skin was flushed by twenty *Mississippi*s when she started the car.

Mr. Blakely was right there when Polly finally opened the door. "That was thirty-nine seconds. I don't know if you're aware of our policy, but the rules clearly state—"

Her mother reached over and slammed the door on his policies. She screeched out of the parking lot while Polly met Mr. Blakely's stunned gaze.

It was hard to stifle her laughter. "Mothers," Polly said.

By second period, word had gotten round about Polly's ragged haircut and dirty jeans. When she walked into Mrs. Finch's debate class, everyone went quiet. Then Carly Leyland burst out laughing.

"Oh my frickin' God," she said.

"Carly!" Mrs. Finch said. "That's quite enough from you."

Olivia avoided Polly's gaze during the heated debate on capital punishment, but after class she was waiting in the hall. She wore lip gloss now, the Carly Leyland variety—extra wet, frosty pink.

"I'll walk with you," Olivia said.

Polly pushed past her. "I don't need your protection."

"I'm not offering it. It's a free country. I can walk where I want."

Polly waved a hand and squinted at the bright, crowded hall. She'd thought it was just Baba's rainbow that was growing brighter, but now she wondered if her own vision was sharpening. Mimi Stigers, the commanding student council president, wore a lion's mane of sapphire blue light around her neck, while Ben Jacobsen, who had lost every election he entered, sported two purple hangdog ears beside his face. Only Olivia's aura looked watered down.

They reached Polly's locker, but Olivia didn't leave.

"What's wrong with you?" Polly asked.

"What's wrong with *you?*"

Polly shielded her hand while she worked the combination, even though Olivia knew it by heart. Olivia's lip quivered as Polly gathered her books.

"Look," Olivia said, her voice shaky. "So I changed my hair. You did too."

Polly slammed her locker shut. "It's not that."

"Well then, what is it? I'm not allowed to be friends with anyone else? I'm supposed to stay lonely and weird like you?"

"That's right! You are!"

The words were out before she could stop them, and Polly turned away from the pity in Olivia's eyes. She had to get out of there, but when she took a step, something slimy and cold hit her in the face.

She cried out, more from shock than pain, as mud trickled down her cheek. Carly Leyland stood three feet away, flicking the last of the sludge from her hands.

"Your makeup looked like it was fading," Carly said. "You wouldn't want to wander around your precious woods looking too clean, would you, Swamp Girl?"

Mimi Stigers looked away. She might have been a lion, but she didn't come to Polly's rescue. No one in the hall moved as Polly struggled not to cry.

"Hey, Liv," Carly said. "Whatcha doing with Swamp Girl?"

"C-Carly," Olivia said, "how could you—"

"Who's your hairstylist?" Carly asked, swatting at Polly's uneven hair. "Frankenstein?"

Joy Lanerson and Crystal Carr looked like Carly's evil minions, laughing hysterically at everything she said. Joy had a lavender aura that faded to gray beside Carly, while Crystal's canary-colored energy hopped around like a nervous bird. Crystal had once come to Baba's house for dogbane tea, a poisonous mixture that might have killed her mother but instead helped shrink the tumor in her brain. In gratitude, Crystal had brought Baba a rare orchid, yet now her hands were muddy too.

Joe Meyer made his way through the crowd and was about to put his arm around Carly when he spotted the dirt on Polly's face.

"Hey," he said. "What's going on?"

Carly leaned in toward Polly and wrinkled her nose. "Maybe I should have put some shit in it. That's what you smell like, Swamp Girl. Shit."

"That's enough," Olivia said.

The light around Carly became a fireworks display of pinks and baby blues. Somehow it made Polly think of a two-year-old in the midst of a tantrum, trying to get everyone to look at her.

"Y-you can't talk to her like that," Olivia went on. "You can't throw dirt at people."

Carly stepped forward. "I can do whatever I want, *Olivia*."

Polly reached out, but Olivia was already gone, running down the hall crying.

Carly rolled her eyes. "Little Miss Crybaby," she said. "God."

The rushing in Polly's ears was so loud, the bell for third period sounded like a whisper. She didn't feel like crying anymore; she was too busy deciding where to aim. She'd never punched anyone in her life, and it turned out she was really, really good at it. Her fist hit Carly's cheek with a satisfying whack, and Carly dropped to her knees. Everyone went quiet, then a couple of the boys called out, "Catfight!"

Polly wished it were a catfight rather than Carly just sitting there holding her cheek and bawling like a baby. Everybody fussed over her until Crystal and Joy finally helped her to her feet.

"I'm feeling a little dizzy," Carly said, feigning a swoon and falling against Joe's chest. Polly couldn't believe anyone took her seriously.

"Let's go tell Mr. Blakely," Joy suggested, glaring at Polly.

Carly acted as if Polly had smashed her legs too, wobbling so badly Joy and Crystal practically had to carry her. But Joe Meyer didn't move. Halfway down the hall, Carly looked over her shoulder at him. "Aren't you coming?"

It was amazing how quickly Carly got her strength back when Joe didn't budge. She threw off her friends' arms and marched over to him. "She just tried to *kill* me," she said.

Joe looked at Carly as if he'd never seen her before. As if this mud-flinging creature had materialized out of thin air. Just whom did he think he'd been kissing?

"You had it coming," Joe said.

The fireworks around Carly exploded. It *was* a little girl that Polly saw around her, petulant and pitiful, the kind who throws mud at you, then screams and cries when you fight back.

"Come on," Carly said, forgetting her dizziness and grabbing Joy and Crystal by the arms. "We're going to see Mr. Blakely."

The crowd slowly dispersed—all except Joe. Polly stole a glance at him, relieved when she couldn't find any similarities between him and his brother, Brad. One was scary, reckless, and not expected to live past twenty-one, while the other was clear-eyed and, from the little she'd seen, surprisingly kind. She wondered if Joe might understand better than anyone the things she'd gone through with Bree. But she also wondered what he was doing with Carly.

"Did your brother get my sister pregnant?" she asked.

Joe leaned back against the lockers, his brown hair falling over his eyes. "Jeez. Give a guy a little warning."

Polly tried to wipe the mud from her cheeks, but it had already caked dry. "Well, did he?" she asked. "Because that's what Carly's been saying."

"I never told her that," he said, and for some reason Polly believed him. She felt soothed by the light around him, all browns and greens, like the rings in a pine log. "But you know how Brad and Bree were. Drugs, stealing stuff, having . . . you know . . . sex."

Polly wanted him to stop talking, and, remarkably, he did. Freckles were coming out on his face now, the way stars do after you've been staring at the sky awhile.

"I'd get so mad at Brad I'd fight him," Joe went on, "even though he always beat the crap out of me. He just laughed me off. It was a joke to him, how far he could fall."

"I don't think it was a joke to Bree," Polly said.

They were quiet, and Polly stood staring at him for so long, he finally said, "Polly?"

She stepped back, blushing, remembering her crazy hair and the mud on her face. Before he could say another word, she turned and ran, wishing the floor would open up and swallow her, wishing she'd run away a second sooner—before she saw him smile.

🦋 🦋 🦋 🦋

Polly's mother was in a meeting, so it was her father who showed up in the principal's office. Mr. Blakely explained the school's zero-tolerance-for-bullying policy and looked at

Polly as if she were a brute. Carly only had to offer a written apology while Polly got two weeks' worth of lunchtime detention in the library, which, she didn't say out loud, was almost a reward.

Out in the parking lot, Polly noticed the sawdust in her dad's hair. People who'd known Paul Greene before said they hardly recognized him now, with his scraggly beard, flannel shirts, and hermit-like existence. No one understood how he could give up a successful law practice to sell woodcarvings. It unnerved people to think that someone could change so much.

But Polly didn't think her dad had changed at all. He'd always been a mountain man; it was just a matter of admitting his true color. Polly was miserable when he left them, but in a weird, mixed-up way, she hadn't really had him until then— until he'd begun to turn a little brown around the edges, more woodlike, solid and sure.

"You're on my side, right?" she said.

Her dad stopped by his pickup. "This isn't about sides, Polly. It's about raising your hand against someone. Violence is never the answer. You know that."

"So I should have just let her throw dirt in my face? I should let her turn Olivia into another person?"

He looked down at his hands. Even in his lawyer days, he'd gone out to the garage whenever the conversation had turned emotional. He preferred stuff he could fix with a hammer and nail.

"If you promise this won't happen again," he said, "I'm willing to keep this from your mother. She doesn't need to worry about this, too."

Polly stepped forward. "See, you do care about her."

"Of course I care. I never said—"

"You could come back then. Take care of her. Come home, Dad. Why don't you come home?"

Her dad took her in his arms, saying, "It's not as easy as that, honey. There were issues, problems we couldn't see our way around. And with Bree . . ."

"Those are just excuses," Polly said. "You're only afraid she won't love you back."

"That's not true," he said. "It's not."

But when Polly pushed him away, she knew that he was lying. She wished that he could see it, his solid brown aura from head to toe, except for a tendril around his mouth that burned pink.

11

ANGELICA

(Angelica)

Legend says angelica got its name when an angel offered it as a cure for the plague, evil spells, and enchantments. The leaves are an ingredient in gin, while the plant relieves cramping and other disorders of the female reproductive tract. Beware! Difficult to distinguish from water hemlock, which can be fatal within fifteen minutes of ingestion.

The morning that Polly's grounding was over, her mom looked in her eyes and said, "I trust you." What that really meant, Polly knew, was *Don't go into the woods*. It meant Polly had to choose between her mom's trust and trying to help Baba.

It was unsettling how quickly she made up her mind. Even if it meant getting grounded again, Polly had to do whatever she could to save her grandmother. Baba was the key to everything, and Polly hadn't seen her out walking or gathering herbs since that night in the grove.

So Polly ignored the blustery November wind and headed straight into the woods after school. Maybe jimsonweed would cure her grandmother, even though it was also capable of causing hallucinations and respiratory arrest. Or tansy, which damaged the liver and digestive tract but treated weak kidneys. It was hard to identify anything in its leafless state, but Polly managed to find both of those plants, plus a red flower that seemed impervious to the weather, its energy shimmering like a summertime mirage.

But it was the field of angelica, frozen in full bloom, that made her heart quicken. The flowers gave off an eerie white light, like the breath of the earth or a gathering of spirits. Polly's grandmother added the angel-winged seeds to her soups and prescribed the root to ease heavy menstrual cramps, but she'd also told Polly that angelica was a gift from the angels. In certain cases, Baba had said, it will heal what no other plant can.

Polly raced to pull three of the plants from the ground, roots and all, and ran down the mountain to Baba's. She found her grandmother in bed, the covers pulled up to her chin. Baba's chest rose and fell steadily, but now even her breath was rainbow-colored. Polly quickly took off her backpack and laid out her plants on the bed.

The white glow of the angelica was already dimming to a thin gray pallor, while the red flower that had been so brilliant in the woods gave off no shimmer at all. Polly ran for water, but by the time she got back with a full vase the last of the light had gone from the angelica. Baba had woken and was struggling to sit up, her gaze going first to the limp blossoms, then to Polly's stricken face. She read her secret in a heartbeat.

"You can't save everyone," she said, and Polly began to cry.

❦ ❦ ❦ ❦

Two months after Bree had gone, it was just as Polly had predicted. The neighbors avoided them, no one said Bree's name, and the police reluctantly admitted that the case of Brianna Greene had gone cold. Yet out of the blue Polly's mom made an elaborate Thanksgiving dinner—turkey, mashed potatoes, cranberries, the works. It was Polly's favorite meal, but when she sat at the table she felt reluctant to eat it, as if it was wrong to have such abundance when Bree had nothing.

"I guess I haven't quite figured out how to cook for two," Polly's mom said, looking guilty herself as she played with a mountain of potatoes on her plate. Then, very deliberately, she took her first bite.

Polly cut up her turkey and ate it, ashamed at how good it was.

"I was thinking," her mother went on. "Maybe you'd like to go to your dad's this weekend."

Polly looked up. She hadn't been to her dad's cabin since Bree left. "Really?"

Her mom stopped eating, but she looked Polly in the eye. "Really," she said.

� � �

The next day, Polly's dad pulled up in front of the house. "Ah," he said, "it's the lovely fairy Gwendolyn."

Polly felt so happy, it was almost indecent. She was going to the cabin, to the *woods*. But when she got in the truck, her dad headed toward town.

"I've got a surprise for you," he said.

Polly thought they might be going for ice cream, the way they used to every weekend, but instead he turned down Olivia's street. Polly's stomach lurched when he came to a stop in the Nelsons' driveway.

"I told her to bring a sleeping bag," her dad said. "You two can sleep in the loft."

"What do you mean?" Polly asked. "She agreed to come?"

Olivia walked out the door with her sleeping bag and pink overnight case. Polly's dad opened the door to the pickup, saying, "Ladies, I believe you've met."

Olivia stuffed her things behind the seat while Polly slid over to make room in the cab. Polly had no idea what to say, and apparently Olivia didn't either. She got in beside her and turned to the window as Polly's dad headed toward the woods.

They drove past the Mountain Winds construction office, then onto the bumpy dirt road that led to the cabin, every squeak of the truck sounding like a shout. Even Polly's dad, who could go days without speaking, kept glancing over to see if they were all right.

"Supposed to be a warm winter," he said at last.

When the truck hit a pothole, Olivia elbowed Polly in the ribs. "I read that too," Olivia said, her face all innocence. "In the *Farmers' Almanac*. Unusually warm, then wet and snowy later." She kicked Polly under the seat.

Polly's dad was oblivious, launching into a discussion of the last seven years of drought, while Polly turned, ready to fight. But instead of a battle, she found Olivia aiming a finger at her knee, where she knew Polly was most ticklish. Suddenly, the horrible, heavy thing that had been lodged in Polly's chest disappeared.

"You never know," her dad said. "Every once in a while winter just passes us by."

Polly grabbed Olivia's hand before she could tickle her, but the two of them still burst out laughing.

"I didn't realize the weather was so funny," her dad went on.

They laughed harder, and when another bump entangled their arms, they left them that way. Polly's dad shook his head and turned on the radio, but beneath his beard, Polly could tell, he was smiling too.

❦ ❦ ❦ ❦

The cabin sat in a pretty little bowl, with Sheep Creek and a gentle rise on one side and a steep, wooded incline on the other. Except for the sunny vegetable garden, the land was densely shaded, the oldest pines in the area well over a hundred feet tall.

There was no electricity or phone line in the cabin. The refrigerator, stove, and lights ran on propane from a giant tank in the back. It was so quiet, Polly always took out the battery from her wristwatch. The ticking seemed out of place.

Polly dragged Olivia inside. Except for the grove and Baba's house, the cabin was Polly's favorite place on earth. Even on the hottest summer days, the interior was cool. The walls and ceiling were smoothed logs still oozing with sap, the floor hand-hewn Douglas fir, the countertops and cabinets pine. It was like stepping inside a tree. There was one large room on the main floor and a loft upstairs. The air always smelled of huckleberry pancakes.

That afternoon, Polly and Olivia watched her dad work. He used an awl and chisel to carve an eight-foot-long trunk of larch, one of the many he found downed in the woods after windstorms. He had never cut down a living tree.

"What are you making?" Polly asked, running her hands down the smoothed sides of the wood where he'd already cut in long, gentle curves.

Her father had sawdust in his beard again as he looked at the wood. "A girl."

❧ ❧ ❧ ❧

Polly relished the chance to get into the forest again. Her mom could hardly complain when it was Polly's dad who suggested they go for a walk after dinner. The three of them put on their jackets and gloves and headed into the woods.

The air was bone-chilling and calm, the way it always was before the first real snow. Polly heard a creature, probably a squirrel, rustling in the bushes for warmth. Then her dad moved in front of them.

"Be still," he whispered.

A growl came from their left, and Polly sensed something coming up behind them. A pack, she thought, moving in stealthily to surround them. Then, as if on some signal, the wolves emerged from the trees.

They were gray wolves, Polly knew, from one of the packs reintroduced to Idaho, but they weren't gray. Their fur ranged from white to silver to black to rust. The biggest one was black and stood menacingly to the left, while a smaller tan wolf took her place beside him. The alpha male and female,

Polly thought, with the female the obvious warrior. There was a slash mark across her wide muzzle and dried blood on her fur. She had round, erect ears; a long, straight tail held up nearly vertical; and the most massive paws Polly had ever seen.

A cold breeze brushed across Polly's face, but the rest of her was on fire. How Baba would have loved to see them! So regal, bold, and proud, everything wild things should be. Polly's heart raced in awe and fear, but also in a strange need to protect them. She'd seen the celebrations on the news when the wolves were taken off the endangered-species list, and the rush of men eager to buy hunting tags. The elk herds were down, the wolves preyed on cattle and sheep, and ranchers wanted justice. Like Baba, the wolves were blamed when anything went wrong.

The largest wolf bared his teeth, and another growled. Polly's dad looked behind them, but they were surrounded.

Then another wolf, far smaller than the others, raced out of the woods, tail wagging. Gray and black, he ran in circles joyfully until the black male lunged and took him by the throat. The small wolf yelped, and Olivia cried out. The animal looked lifeless—until the leader let go and the younger wolf leaped to his feet, his tail still wagging, as if it had all been in fun.

The other wolves did nothing, though Polly had the feeling that if they'd been human, they would have rolled their eyes. Then, in a split second, the young wolf turned and came barreling at Polly. She screamed, expecting the sharp sting of fangs in her throat, but instead got only paws on her shoulders and a wet tongue on her face. The animal stood on its hind legs and licked her madly.

"Bronco?" she said.

The dog's tail wagged exuberantly, and the pack, as if respecting even a crazy dog's loyalties, slipped soundlessly back into the woods. Bronco licked her once more, then ran off, barking happily as he disappeared behind the trees. Polly laughed in relief and wonder. His fur had come in thick and glossy, and Polly imagined him bounding through the woods, sleeping soundly against his new furry siblings, getting nipped but never getting chained or beaten. Part of a pack, yet free. A wild thing.

"Did you see that?" Olivia said, her eyes shining. "Wolves. Oh, Polly, *wolves.*"

❦ ❦ ❦ ❦

That night Polly and Olivia rolled out sleeping bags in the loft while Polly's dad slept on the couch downstairs. They spoke of teachers and tests, until Polly's dad started to snore.

"Olivia?" Polly whispered. "Where do you think Bree is? Honestly."

Olivia burrowed down in her sleeping bag. "I think she went into the woods like she told you she would, but she left before it got too cold. Maybe she's in some city."

Polly looked out the window, where a curtain of clouds blocked the moon. "I think she's out there. I really do. And I think my grandmother is helping her."

Olivia hesitated, then said softly, "Would she do that, Polly? Break your mom's heart that way?"

Polly shook her head. "I don't know. Maybe, if she thought it was the only way to save Bree. Some of her medicines are worse than the symptoms they treat. Baba's never been afraid to hurt people if it means she can get them well."

Polly closed her eyes as they lay in silence. She didn't want to talk about Bree anymore, so she told Olivia the story of Gwendolyn the woodland fairy, ending the tale in the usual place, where her dad had left off. The part where Gwendolyn had to search for Fairyland in the only place she hadn't looked—the Dark Lands.

"Then what happened?" Olivia asked.

Polly had given her dad months to finish the story, but it was obvious he'd forgotten all about it. She had no choice but to write the ending herself.

"Gwendolyn walked and walked, and every day the forest got darker," she said. "Soon it was black as night all the time and she could only stumble forward, hands held out in front of her like a blind woman. The trunks of the trees felt like flesh. Instead of the rustling of leaves, she heard moans and sighs. She could find no food and water, and she began to grow weak."

In the darkness, Polly saw the whites of Olivia's eyes.

"The trees moved beside her now," Polly went on, "tripping her, tugging her hair, entangling her in their branches. There was no end to the darkness. And Gwendolyn realized there was no way out."

Olivia sat up. "What happened to her?"

Polly hadn't known herself until that moment. Until she remembered the sound of Baba's voice in the forest.

"She began to sing," she said. "An old folk song her grand-mother had taught her." Polly cleared her throat, and began to sing too.

The bridal-songs and cradle-songs have cadences of sorrow,
The laughter of the sun to-day, the wind of earth to-morrow.
Far sweeter sound the forest-notes where forest-streams are
 falling;
O mother mine, I cannot stay, the fairy-folk are calling.

Olivia grabbed Polly's hand. "Did she find Fairyland?"

Polly smiled, knowing the ending now and glad that she'd discovered it on her own. "Of course," she said. "She just had to go through the dark for a bit."

❦ ❦ ❦ ❦

The snow had started falling during Polly's story. The girls got up and stood at the window, looking out at the blanket of white.

"What do you think the wolves are doing?" Olivia asked, pressing her palms against the glass.

"I'll bet they're long gone by now," Polly said.

Olivia turned from the window. "I'm not afraid of them. Isn't that weird? I'm afraid of everything, but not of wolves. Let's go outside."

Polly stared at her friend's bright eyes, then out at the frosted woods. If her father woke to find them gone, she'd lose his trust for good, yet the forest had never looked as beautiful. It was like a wonderland out there, a land of white bears, wolves, and ice. Polly grabbed Olivia's hand and led her downstairs. Quietly putting on their jackets and boots, they slipped out the front door as Polly's dad went on snoring.

There were no wolf tracks in the snow, and no plants Polly could bring to Bree. Then she remembered the garden vegetables she'd canned with her father that summer. She ran to the storage shed for a jar of carrots and pickled beets and smiled devilishly as she chose two containers of green beans for Olivia to carry. She could picture Bree gagging as she ate them—Bree had always hated green vegetables.

"Why do we need—"

"For Bree," Polly said.

"But how will she find them? Where should we leave them?"

Polly led her into the trees. She usually came to the grove from the other side of the mountain, but she was confident that she could find her way. A few times she had to stop to get her bearings, not an easy thing to do in the darkness and worsening snow, but eventually they made it to the wall of devil's club. The leaves had all fallen from the shrub, yet the tangle of stems and thorns was just as dense and forbidding. Nothing could be seen of the grove on the other side. It took Polly three passes to find the opening.

"Follow me," she said.

She and Olivia slithered beneath the thorny plant, and as soon as they entered the larch grove, they saw the campfire blazing.

"Whoa," Olivia said. Snow covered the ground, except beneath the larches, where it was heaped with golden needles. "What is this place? Who's here?"

A log crackled as if it had just been thrown on the flames, yet Polly saw no one. "It's Bree's fire," she said.

Olivia looked around, squinting to see into the darkness beyond the trees. "Really? Why doesn't she come out?"

Polly wished she knew the answer. "I don't know. She's Bree. Let's leave the vegetables over there, on the boulder."

They set down the jars and brushed away snow to sit by

the fire. Polly brushed aside the matchbook, now soggy and unusable. It was a well-built blaze, with enough wood set aside to burn all night.

"Do you believe in magic?" Polly asked after a long silence.

Olivia must have felt as safe in the grove as Polly did, because she yawned. "It seems unlikely."

"Yeah."

"It's like everything you believe in when you're little turns out to be a lie."

Polly nodded. The truth was like stars going out. First the Easter Bunny, then the Tooth Fairy, then Santa Claus. What next? What happened when everything went dark?

But everything *didn't* go dark. That's what Polly wanted to say. Olivia herself lit up the night. Polly had been wrong about her before. Olivia's aura wasn't watered down at all; it was camouflaged, like a wolf's coat of tan, silver, and gold.

"Olivia?" Polly said. "Can I tell you something?"

Olivia nodded, watching the snow sizzle as it hit the flames.

"I see things around people. Auras, I guess. Colors, even shapes."

Polly tensed, steeling herself for Olivia's scorn, but all Olivia said was "Why didn't you ever tell me before? D-do you see anything around me?"

Polly's eyes watered, surprised at how much it meant to be believed.

"A wolf," she said. "I think I see a wolf."

Plenty of people would have been horrified by Polly's vision, but Olivia searched her face to make sure it was the truth. It was as if she'd never looked in a mirror and Polly had had to tell her what she saw: a girl who was loyal, proud, and much braver than anyone thought.

"Really?" Olivia said. "A wolf?"

Polly laughed. "With silver and gold fur. You should see it."

They talked for a while of the things Polly saw, then settled into a comfortable silence. Polly swore she never closed her eyes, yet she dreamed. The larches no longer swayed, but walked. Faces emerged from the knots, hips and breasts grew from nubs, shapely legs split from trunks. The trees became beautiful dryads, their branches replaced with fingers, bark stretching into skin and long, wild hair. They greeted one another with long embraces and laughter, admiring each other's transformations, twirling bodies that gleamed like polished wood.

And from the bark of the largest tree, Baba's favorite, came Polly's grandmother.

Polly should have been stunned, but she wasn't. She felt only comfort and staggering happiness, as if now, at last, everything was as it should be. The dryads surrounded her and Olivia, marveling over them, laughing, caressing them as if they were newborns, soft and perfect. They massaged their arms, rubbed their feet, sang a lovely foreign song, with words Polly couldn't understand but knew was a lullaby. The last thing she remembered was the scent of cedar in the air.

When she woke at dawn beside Olivia, the snow was six inches deep, and she still smelled the luscious scent of the larches, of Baba.

"Polly?" Olivia said, awake now too and staring wide-eyed at the trees, then over at the boulder where the vegetable jars had disappeared, except for the green beans.

Don't say it, Polly thought. *Don't say it was a dream.*

At last Olivia turned to Polly.

"You know what we should call this place? Girlwood."

The snow dropped from one of the branches, as if the larches agreed.

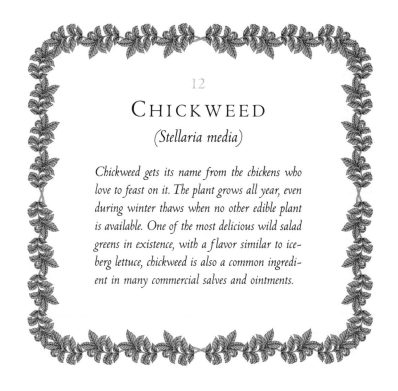

12

CHICKWEED

(Stellaria media)

Chickweed gets its name from the chickens who love to feast on it. The plant grows all year, even during winter thaws when no other edible plant is available. One of the most delicious wild salad greens in existence, with a flavor similar to iceberg lettuce, chickweed is also a common ingredient in many commercial salves and ointments.

The forest could have been Fairyland as Polly and Olivia walked home from Girlwood—the dawn sky like a field of tulips, the new snow twinkling pink, green, and blue, as if even the ground they walked on was enchanted.

Polly's dad was sitting on the porch stoop when they approached, his face unreadable.

"Dad," Polly said, "I'm so s—"

"I'll always worry about you," he said. "Even when you're

sixty. Every time you're late, I'll imagine what it's like to lose you. I can't go through that again, Polly."

Polly sat beside him, his quiet, pained voice worse than shouting. "But you don't have to worry," she said. "I'm the one who stayed."

He closed his eyes a moment, then kissed her bird's-nest hair. "I know, honey."

Olivia joined them on the stoop. Polly didn't think her dad would believe the whole truth, but she wanted to offer him something. So she told him about the canned vegetables they'd left for Bree.

"She took them," she said. "Everything but the green beans."

People got nervous because her dad was so silent now, but all Polly cared about was that he start believing her. He stared at her for a good minute, then finally said, "We combed the woods. The police refuse to look there anymore. They won't look anywhere unless they get a tip."

"Baba says all you need to survive is water, food, and shelter. There are hot springs in the woods where the water never freezes. If Bree could find a cabin or some other shelter, all she'd need is food. We can give her that."

He looked toward the woods. "She's just a girl, Polly," he said.

Both Polly and Olivia gasped. Polly jumped to her feet. "So?"

"Sweetheart, I'm just saying—"

"I know what you're saying. You and Mom both. But at least Mom goes out and leaves things for her, even if she doesn't really believe Bree is there."

Her dad squinted into the sun as it came up through the trees. "Your mom's been leaving things for Bree?"

"Of course! Clothes, boots, food. At least she's doing *something*."

Her father looked like someone who'd just been told the sun came up in the west, not the east, that everything he thought he knew was wrong. "Your mother shouldn't be out there alone," he said, then he headed around back to the woodpile. When Polly and Olivia followed, he grabbed an ax and split a twenty-inch round cleanly in half. "It would have been a death wish for Bree to go into the woods," he said. "A slap in the face of the people who love her."

Polly could have told him that Bree probably hadn't even considered them, but he kept swinging.

"If she did go into the woods," he went on, "do you know how much wood it would take to keep her warm this winter?" Though his voice was pained, the brown glow around him was growing stronger.

He set up a line of pine rounds and split them one after the other, wood chips flying around him like shrapnel. Polly had to hide her smile as she led Olivia away.

The following Monday, Mrs. Finch asked the class to choose a topic for debate. Polly usually stayed silent, but this time she raised her hand.

"Yes?" Mrs. Finch said encouragingly. "Polly?"

"How about Mountain Winds?"

The smile faded from Mrs. Finch's face as Carly Leyland looked up from her desk. "What do you mean?" the teacher asked.

"You know," Polly said. "A debate on whether or not it's right to hack up a mountain so a few rich people can enjoy the view."

The class got real quiet, and then Carly Leyland stood. "I'll take pro," she said, and Mason Halberton hooted.

Mrs. Finch studied Polly as if she'd never seen her before. "You'll take con?"

Polly swallowed. "Yes."

"All right," Mrs. Finch said, though she didn't sound too sure. "Everyone choose sides and write your arguments. Polly and Carly will present them in twenty minutes."

Polly kept her head down. She didn't expect anyone to side with a swamp girl, but as she took out her spiral notebook she heard shuffling. Olivia was coming her way, along with Mandy Aloman and Bridget Stork. Then John Bender, who lived in a cabin without electricity much like Polly's dad's, and Peter Wendell, a shy, acne-ridden boy with an aura as vivid and blue as a tropical sea.

"Wow," Polly said. "I didn't think . . . Thanks."

The light around John Bender was like a turtle shell, olive green and ribbed. Kids made fun of the crude cabin he lived in, but Polly envied his thousand-acre backyard. When Mountain Winds was built, he'd have millionaires for neighbors but fences shutting him out of his favorite trails.

They composed their arguments, and twenty minutes later, Mrs. Finch called Carly and Polly to the front of the class. Carly was getting an A and Polly a C− in debate, which was probably the reason that Carly had such a bright smile.

"Miss Leyland," Mrs. Finch said, "the pros begin."

Carly stepped forward in her skirt and creamy blue sweater, and everyone grinned at her foolishly. She was so pretty, Polly thought, it put people in a stupor.

"Mountain Winds," she began. "Heaven on Earth."

She paused for effect, and Polly rolled her eyes. Carly had merely memorized the slogan on her dad's signs and brochures.

"One of the most basic needs is a place to live," Carly continued. "My father has been a hard-working developer in Idaho for twenty years. He's nothing fancy. He's never done anything more than put in ten thousand homes for everyday people. And now he wants to do more. We've all seen the local woods. The pines have been eaten up by beetles, the whole forest is overgrown and diseased. One lightning strike, one fire, and we'll lose it all. We can't afford to do nothing!"

Carly smiled while the class whispered. "My dad's *saving* the woods," she went on. "He's taking out the diseased timber and thinning the trees until the forest is pretty again, and safe. Any other developer would raze the whole mountain and build condominiums. *My* dad's going to leave open space and even put in a swimming pool! He's the good guy here."

When she was through, the applause was deafening. Polly looked at her notes and felt sick. Her team had forgotten the first rule of debate: focus on facts, not emotion. They'd wasted twenty minutes coming up with nothing more than wishes, their desire that something in this world remain wild and untouched and a refuge for those who needed it— whether they were fairies or wolves or girls.

Polly stepped forward. "I want to talk . . ." Her voice broke, and the girls in the front row laughed. She cleared her throat and tried again.

"I want to talk about the trees." She hoped no one noticed her trembling, though it was violent enough to flutter the paper in her hand. "Carly's right about one thing. They *are* diseased, and many of them are dying. But that's what they're *supposed* to do. Trees get sick and die, forest fires burn them to the ground, and stronger stands grow up through the ashes. That's the *plan*. We get so wrapped up in fixing things, managing things, it's like we forget we're not in charge! The trouble isn't pine beetles or fires but us, building houses where they were never meant to go, always meddling and screwing things up."

The kids in the front row were opening and closing their mouths in silent mockery, then falling all over one another in hysterics. Even as Mrs. Finch told them to quiet down, a bead of sweat trickled down Polly's spine. She looked at her notes once again, then crumpled them in her hand.

"Do you think magic is real?" Polly asked.

The words just popped out, and half the class, including Carly, snickered. Polly forgot what she'd been going to say next and stared at the floor, where someone had dropped a chewed pencil on the old green linoleum. Her eyes were burning, and it took her a moment to realize what she was seeing. A few inches away, the floor was gray, yet when she moved a foot, the greenish hue went with her. The color, it seemed, was coming from her.

Polly blinked a few times to make sure the light didn't vanish. She'd never looked for her own aura, afraid that it would be some dull color or perhaps not be there at all, but now she wondered how she'd ever missed the green tendrils emanating from her skin. She was the color of the firs, of the larches in summer, of Baba. She raised her head and smiled at Olivia.

"Magic is all the things we don't understand and aren't meant to," she went on. "It's the best things, like chickweed that grows in the middle of winter when the elk are starving or a bear that opens its eyes on the first day of spring. Magic is a forest that can heal itself, and everything in it, if we don't tear it down first."

The class got a little quieter. "Carly says it could be worse," Polly continued, her voice growing steadier. "And she's right. It could be two thousand houses instead of one thousand. It could be another clear-cut. But is that what we're going to settle for? A life that could be worse? Carly says they're going to clean up the woods, but did you know they're going to put up a gate too? I read it in their brochure. You'll need a code to get in."

There were rumblings in the class, and the sweat on Polly's neck began to cool.

"This is just phase one," she said, raising her voice to be heard. "Then they'll want to build up the next ridge. And the next. What's going to happen when we're grown up and want to come home to camp or fish or just take a walk in the woods? I'll tell you what will happen. We'll be out of luck. The woods will be cut down, paved over, and gated off. And only Carly Leyland will have the key to get in. We'll be forty years old and still praying she likes us enough to invite us over."

The room was hushed as Mrs. Finch turned to Carly. "Do you have a rebuttal?"

Carly tossed her own notes in the trash. "I'd just like to make sure everyone knows where Polly's dad lives," she said. "In a *cabin*, in her precious *woods*. Why does he get to live there and nobody else?"

"That cabin's been there for sixty years," Polly said.

"So what? What happens if a fire comes through and threatens his house?"

"If the cabin burns, it burns," Polly said. "That's the chance he's taking."

"Oh, right. You'd call the fire department in a second, make them chop down all the trees just to keep him safe."

"I would not! My dad doesn't even own a phone."

Carly rolled her eyes. "Yeah. We know all about your dad. Mr. Off-the-Grid Granola. Another nut case like your grandmother. At least he doesn't go around poisoning people."

"My grandma doesn't poison people!" Polly said. "She heals them. What do you know about my family?"

"I know everybody in it leaves."

"Carly!" Mrs. Finch said. "Stick to the topic, please."

The bell rang but no one moved. Even the boys who would have ordinarily called out "Catfight!" were silent.

"This is all because of your sister," Carly hissed at Polly. The kids in the back row practically fell over their desks to listen. "I heard that you think she's out there somewhere, living off the land. Give me a break! Brianna Greene couldn't survive a day without a roof over her head and a needle in her arm. She was a drug addict, and everyone knew it. She was going to die anyway."

A boy from the next class came in as Polly's face went pale. He looked at the shell-shocked students in the room, then at Mrs. Finch.

"Is this third period or what?"

Carly snatched her notebook and flounced out of class. *Just don't cry,* Polly told herself again. It could be her own slogan. *Just don't cry.*

Joy Lanerson might have touched Polly's arm as she left, though it was over too quick to know for sure. Olivia, Mandy, and Bridget surrounded her.

"She is so cruel," Mandy said.

Polly's tears had backed up, creating a logjam in her throat, but she squared her shoulders and turned to her friends. *Her* friends. She wasn't alone anymore.

"Meet me by the creek after school," Polly said. "There's something I want to show you."

13

ELK (EVERT'S) THISTLE
(Cirsium scariosum)

Thorny, invasive elk thistle has been called the curse of the earth, yet thistle has extensive edible and medicinal uses. Found in wet soil in meadows and gardens, the plant has tender spring stems that have a sweet taste and can be eaten raw after the spiny covering is peeled away. Thistle treats respiratory congestion and infections.

After school, Polly met Olivia, Mandy, and Bridget by the swollen creek. A few days of mild, sunny weather had turned the snowy streets to slush. The steep hill behind Baba's was now slick with mud, so Polly and the girls put on their light jackets and boots and headed the long way around, past the mushy, tangled banks of Sheep Creek and out toward the future entrance of Mountain Winds. Workers were there installing a massive rock waterfall, and chain saws buzzed in the distance. Occasionally a tree thudded against the earth, sending shock waves beneath their feet.

Polly hoped to creep past the double-wide trailer unnoticed, but something about the figure huddled on the stairs caught her attention. Not the blond hair or blue sweater, but the slumped shoulders. Carly Leyland, with her head in her hands.

"Is that—"

Carly lifted her head when Olivia spoke. Polly froze, unable to walk away from the sight of Carly Leyland *crying*, but not about to help her either. Carly rushed inside the trailer, only to be escorted back out a moment later by a stocky, square-faced man.

"For God's sake, Carly," he said, manhandling her down the stairs. "I told you to go home and talk to your mother. I've got *buyers* here."

Carly blushed furiously, but what really surprised Polly was the way her aura shrank when her father leaned in and, at one point, disappeared. It was like getting a glimpse of something she shouldn't see—the way a family treated each other when they thought no one was looking.

"Excuse me?" Polly said, hurrying forward. "Mr. Leyland? Do you have a minute to talk? We had a debate at school about Mountain Winds and we thought—"

The look of scorn on his face stopped her.

"Do you really think I've got time to talk to a bunch of kids?" he asked. "Run away and play, would you? I'm selling lots here."

He went into the trailer and slammed the door. *This* was the dad Carly gushed about and admired? A salesman in a cheesy plaid sport coat?

"This is private property." Carly sniffled. "Didn't you see the signs?"

Indeed there were NO TRESPASSING signs nailed into a dozen trees now. So much for a development that would be open to the whole community.

"Carly," Olivia said, "we were just—"

Carly brushed back a tear and extended her arm like a traffic cop. "Talk to the hand, Liv."

She looked so ridiculous with her hand out that Polly almost felt sorry for her.

"Let's go," Polly said softly to her friends, leading them past the NO TRESPASSING signs, knowing Carly couldn't rat on them. Her father was with his buyers. It might be hours before he gave his own daughter the time of day.

꽃 꽃 꽃 꽃

The chain saws were a distant hum by the time they reached the devil's club.

"Weird," Bridget said, looking like an explorer in her cargo pants and khaki jacket. "Like barbed wire."

Despite the mud and slush, Polly got on her belly and slithered into the opening.

"I'll never fit through there," Mandy said.

Polly hadn't thought about the narrow tunnel and Mandy's size, but now it seemed like a test. Was this place magical or wasn't it? "Just follow me."

"Polly!"

Polly crawled through the tunnel and into the larch grove, where even the jars of green beans had disappeared. She smiled, imagining Bree's puckered face when she ate them. Next, Polly would bring peas, which Bree hated even more. She'd find that cabin Baba had talked about and set out the jars like a trail of bread crumbs. Baba wasn't the only one who could help Bree now.

Olivia came next in her rumpled beige coat, then skinny Bridget, but there was no sign of Mandy. Polly was just crouching down to go back for her when a round face poked through the vines of the devil's club.

"I fit!" Mandy said.

She got to her feet and brushed the dirt off her pants, not realizing that she was skimming her fingers through an aura as sleek and iridescent as a mermaid's tail. Outside of Girlwood, Polly hardly noticed Mandy's aura at all, but in the grove it was a deep ocean blue. As the girls gawked at the towering larches, Polly decided that magic was not rare at all, but so common people overlooked it. It was everywhere, in everything, all the time.

Mandy leaned back to see to the top of Baba's favorite tree. "I didn't notice these trees when we were walking up here."

"You didn't see them," Polly said. "You can't."

The girls looked at her. "That's impossible," Bridget said.

"Yeah, well, go out there and tell me if you can see them."

Bridget did just that. She slithered back through the thorny tunnel and marched around outside the devil's club. A few minutes later she came back, looking mystified.

"Double weird," she said. "Maybe we're on a downslope and don't realize it."

Polly didn't answer. She picked up the bow and drill she'd left by the fire pit and went through the same steps she'd followed with Baba—setting up the firewood in the ring, gathering any dry grasses and needles she could find for tinder, then sawing the bow back and forth in a steady rhythm. Everything was still wet from last week's snow, but Polly knew the worst thing she could do was give up too soon. Twenty minutes later, she was still sawing despite the ache in her arm and the girls' complaining of boredom. Finally, she drew back and found the ember on the fireboard. Transferring it carefully to her tinder, she blew until the smoke turned to flame.

When Polly looked up, Bridget's aura had deepened to the darkest purple, the color of a raven's feathers.

"Where did you learn to do that?" Bridget asked.

Polly shrugged, but she was flushed with pride. She could keep her friends warm. It wasn't beauty or popularity or Baba's gift with plants, but it was still a kind of power.

"They haven't tagged these trees for thinning," Bridget said, wandering through the grove.

Polly smiled. "I don't think the Leylands know about this place."

"But it's in the middle of Mountain Winds," Bridget pointed out. "They have to know."

Mandy stood close to the fire, her cheeks still rosy from the cold but the rest of her bathed in a watery blue light. Polly wouldn't be surprised if she slept on silk sheets or could hold her breath for longer than was humanly possible. She wouldn't be surprised by anything anymore.

"Well," Polly said. "They don't."

Olivia looked around nervously. "Do you think this place is haunted?" she asked.

"Not haunted," Polly said. "Alive."

They all went quiet, then Mandy said, "I've got goose bumps."

"Yeah. Me too."

"Me too."

"We call it Girlwood," Olivia said.

"You can't tell anyone about this place," Polly added. "Not even your parents. If anyone else finds it, they'll ruin it."

Bridget and Mandy looked at the larches as if they were listening in, then nodded solemnly.

"That's settled then," Polly said. "Let's find something to eat."

The pickings were slim. Polly found only a few mealy serviceberries, along with black lichen and elk thistle roots.

"You mean eat this stuff?" Mandy asked, looking skeptically at the plants Polly put in her hand.

"We learned about elk thistle in Girl Scouts," Bridget said. "This guy survived on the roots for a month when he was lost in Yellowstone without his glasses."

"He survived on *this?*" Mandy poked at the dirty root as if it were a dead bug.

Olivia bit into the root and managed to swallow. "Not as bad as broccoli," she said.

Polly laughed. Bridget ate the root whole, while Mandy took a polite bite and tried not to gag. They devoured the berries and sampled a few strands of the lichen.

"Ugh," Mandy said. "Tastes like dirt."

"How do you even know what dirt tastes like?" Bridget asked.

Mandy blushed as Polly piled more wood on the fire.

"Won't someone see the smoke?" Olivia asked.

They stopped for a moment and listened. They'd forgotten about the chain saws and now had to strain to hear them.

"I don't think they can see it," Polly said. "I think the larch trees are hidden, and everything and everyone in here is safe."

Polly braced herself when they all went quiet. She knew how crazy and impossible it sounded. The girls watched the fire, then finally Bridget said, "Cool."

Polly could have hugged her, but instead she offered a secret. "Bree's out here," she said. "I leave food for her on that boulder over there. Elk thistle, elderberries, sheep sorrel, whatever I can find. People think she can't survive, but she can." Her friends stared at her and she struggled to catch her breath. "The magic's in her, too."

They all looked around the grove. When no one said anything to refute her, Polly thought that maybe the greatest kindness friends can offer is their silence. Whole minutes, hours, or even lifetimes when they don't laugh or call you a fool.

"Food is one thing," Bridget said, "but what Bree needs is shelter."

She began braiding her long hair. Her fingers were deft, and when she was through, she looked like another person— with high cheekbones Polly had never seen before and glittering, raven eyes.

Bridget kicked at the slush, looking for fallen branches. "We can make a hut," she said. "If we position it between two of the larches, we can use their trunks as our side poles and their branches to support a ridgepole. That's the top of our ceiling."

"Girl Scouts again?" Polly asked.

Bridget smiled. "It was a good troop."

They all searched for branches and followed Bridget's directions for a simple lean-to. First, they chose two larches, eight feet apart, to serve as their side poles, then the four of them dragged over a ten-foot-long log. It was eight inches wide and soaking wet, but Bridget was already thinking ahead, using their jackets like slings. With a little tree climbing and more muscle strength than they'd ever shown in gym class, the girls hoisted the log seven feet up into the forked branches of the larches. With the trees as their side poles and the ceiling beam in place, their shelter began to take shape.

Bridget did most of the work, gathering dozens of support poles—branches about twelve feet long—and laying them at forty-five-degree angles from the ridgepole. She stepped back to inspect her progress. The lean-to would be a simple inverted *V*.

"We'll leave this part open for a doorway," she said. "We can strengthen everything later, but right now it's more important that Bree has a roof."

She instructed them to gather moss, boughs, and bark. As they brought her the materials, she began layering them from bottom to top over the support poles. Boughs first, then bark and moss, overlapping every section as if she were laying shingles. By the time dusk arrived, their lean-to was covered and snug.

After a final inspection by Bridget, the girls went inside the makeshift hut, which turned out to be big enough for all of them. Their heads didn't even hit the ceiling. Rain couldn't get to them, the walls broke the wind, and no one spoke. It was almost too much to believe that four twelve-year-olds, four *girls*, could make fire, find their own food, and build a shelter.

They squeezed one another's hands the moment they realized it: they were the girls of Girlwood. There was nothing they couldn't do.

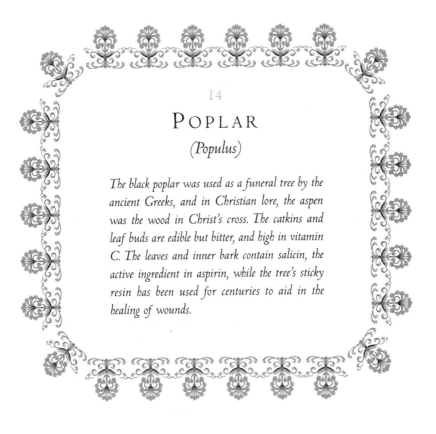

14

POPLAR
(Populus)

The black poplar was used as a funeral tree by the ancient Greeks, and in Christian lore, the aspen was the wood in Christ's cross. The catkins and leaf buds are edible but bitter, and high in vitamin C. The leaves and inner bark contain salicin, the active ingredient in aspirin, while the tree's sticky resin has been used for centuries to aid in the healing of wounds.

*B*ridget told her parents there was a new afterschool chess club, Mandy and Olivia pleaded choir, and Polly pretended she was at Olivia's every day until five. None of them wanted to lie, but somehow they got used to it. They had to protect Girlwood. They had to collect food for Bree and build a bed of leaves and dried grasses in their shelter and make sure the Leyland Corporation never discovered their secret grove.

They were rarely alone in the woods. The storms in early

December were often more rain than snow, and every time the skies cleared the bulldozers and graders raced in to cut roads before the hard freeze. Even when the heavy equipment sat idle, the men trampled through the woods with chain saws, downing all the tagged trees. The girls went quiet when the workers got close, but Polly began to wonder if they could have sung and danced and still remained hidden—as invisible and fairylike as Bree behind the wall of devil's club.

But the magic never stretched beyond the woods. Back behind four walls, sleeping next to the Crying Room, Polly's life was all too ordinary and real. Her mother still muffled her sobs, the dishwasher kept breaking, and, most mundane of all, Polly woke one morning to blood on her sheets. It was no surprise—she was twelve, after all, and most of her friends had started their periods last year—but it wasn't the slightest bit fairylike either. How would Bree cope with *this* in the woods, all the cramps and bloating and blood? Unless Carly Leyland had been right, and Bree was pregnant when she left. In which case, she wouldn't have a period until late spring.

Polly expected her mother to sense what had happened, but even when Polly shoved her sheets in the washing machine, for once doing her own laundry, her mom merely dashed past her, late for a meeting. Polly's stomach cramped as she sat alone at the table and later, as she headed for school, she abruptly changed direction. Her grandmother might not sense anything either, but Polly could count on her to listen. Polly still worried about her health and expected to find her in bed, yet when Polly reached the garden, she found Baba marching out of the cottage, dragging a solid pine chair behind her. There was another bonfire on the driveway, only this time it was furniture that was going up in flames.

Polly raced across the yard. "Baba! What are you doing?"

Her grandmother looked frail, but she was upright and determined, lugging the hefty chair toward the fire.

"I'm getting rid of a few things," she said. "Too much clutter in the house."

In the fire were the charred remains of Baba's coffee table, unfinished bookshelves, and the rack where she'd stored her elderberry wine. Everything she'd owned, it seemed, was made of wood. Baba tipped the chair onto its side, then rolled it into the blaze. The pine wood crackled, and Polly's face burned from the heat.

As the chair ignited, Baba rubbed her hands together, satisfied. "You'll be late for school," she said.

It wasn't an accusation, just a statement of fact. Baba's gaze dropped suddenly to Polly's waist, then rose to her face, softening.

"Ah," she said, opening her arms. "Sweetheart."

Starting her period might have been no big deal, but Polly was surprisingly grateful that Baba had noticed.

"You have a secret inside you now," Baba said, holding her. "Something lush and wild that no one can take away. This is the start of great things, Polly. The start of everything."

Polly felt Baba's arms trembling and said, "You need to sit down."

Baba nodded, but she didn't move. They stood there watching the old chair burn and shoot off red embers like fireworks.

"I had that chair for forty years," Baba said quietly. "Your grandfather bought it for me."

"Then why are you burning it?"

Baba waved a hand. "I never needed a chair to remember him. I don't need much of anything, Polly. Isn't that wonderful?"

"You can't burn all your things, Baba," Polly said.

Her grandmother stood taller. "Well, maybe not all, but most. It's not illegal to burn your furniture, is it?"

"Well, no," Polly said, "but it's . . . strange."

Her grandmother narrowed her gaze until Polly felt guilty for even saying it. Polly shook her head at the fire, but she also smiled. School was starting, but she would just have to be late.

"I'll get the kitchen chairs," Polly said.

Her grandmother was still strong enough to raise her arms and hoot. "Hooray!"

After a few visits to Girlwood, Mandy took a liking to thistle.

"I'm not saying I'd want it for dinner," she said as she chewed on a thorny leaf, "but for food I can find myself, it's not that bad."

Bridget smiled from the shelter that she kept strengthening with more side poles. They'd all noticed that Mandy was losing weight. Every day they came to Girlwood, she was a little slimmer, a little lighter on her feet. And Bridget was growing stronger. To prove that everything they, and Bree, needed was in the grove, she had made an ax by hafting a slender, sharp stone to a two-foot larch branch, and she'd devised a wooden tripod with layers of grass, sand, and charcoal from the fire to filter their stream water. She even came up with an ingenious way to boil off the possible bacteria by pouring small amounts of water into a hollowed-out log and dropping in red hot rocks they'd heated in the fire.

"Is there anything you can't do?" Polly asked her.

"I can't sing."

Just to prove it, she belted out a few horrible bars of "Somewhere Over the Rainbow," and Polly put her hands over her ears. Mandy laughed while Olivia sat on a boulder, looking grim.

"What's wrong?" Polly asked.

Olivia shrugged. "I just wish we could tell our parents where we are, that's all."

"We've been over this," Polly told her. "They'll make us stop coming. They'll freak out about wolves or snowstorms or all the men in the woods."

"Well, there *are* men and snowstorms, and they're building a subdivision around us! My mom'll go berserk if she finds out I've been lying all this time."

"No, she won't," Polly said. "Your mom still reads you bedtime stories. She's like a saint or something. Besides, I've never heard her yell at you once."

Olivia looked away. "That's because I've always been good."

Bridget ignored them and announced her plans for a second shelter. "A wigwam!" she said. "You've got to use saplings, preferably willow so they'll bend. It's a dome shape, basically, and harder to build, but we can make it really big!"

"Let's find some downed willows," Mandy said. "They always grow near water. What's over that way, beyond the larches?"

She and Bridget quickly headed past Baba's tree, where the larches grew in such a dense cluster they seemed to be rising from one giant root. Polly had never explored the boundaries of Girlwood before, not wanting to think that it had an end.

"Come on," Polly said to Olivia, but Olivia didn't budge.

"Polly, I really think we should stop coming here."

"Would you quit saying that? If you'd just stop being so scared all the time—"

"I'm not scared! It's just that my mom says these woods are evil."

"Evil?" Polly said, not sure if she should laugh or be insulted. "Baba practically lives in these woods."

Olivia looked away. "I think that's her point, Polly. I hate to say this, but every Sunday Pastor Bentley has something to say about your grandmother. How she's a witch or something, coming out here to brew potions and cure things even doctors can't. My mom eats up every word."

Polly hardly knew what to say. "Why didn't you tell me your mother felt like that before?"

"What was I supposed to say? I know how you feel about your grandmother, and I don't believe she's evil. As long as we were only around your parents, my mom was okay, but if she caught us here . . ."

Polly couldn't believe it. All this time, when Mrs. Nelson had been calling her "honey" and getting her extra blankets when she slept over, she'd really been watching her for signs of witchery, peeking in while she slept to see if she'd sprouted horns.

"Polly?" Olivia said.

"Let's go. I don't want to lose them."

Polly's eyes burned as she followed Bridget and Mandy's trail. What if Olivia started to hate her too? Obviously, it was as easy as listening to what someone told you. As simple as not trusting yourself enough to make up your own mind.

"Polly!" Olivia said.

Polly didn't look back as she climbed over a decaying trunk. Then all at once, the woods stopped, and she blinked at the light.

The grove ended at a cliff. Mandy and Bridget stood on the precipice looking down a nearly vertical slope of snow and rock. At the bottom was a fast-moving river, and just beyond it, the steep, north-facing wall of the canyon, wet and slick with moss.

Olivia came up behind her, and the four girls looked down at the survey stakes at the bottom of the ravine. There was nothing to say. It was a wild and perfect place, and it would be ruined.

"I'll bet those are willows growing near the stream," Mandy said, and before they could tell her the cliff was too steep and it would take hours to climb back up, she was on her bottom. The old Mandy would have launched an avalanche of snow and rocks, but this new lighter girl barely skimmed the surface of the slope as she slid safely to the canyon floor.

"Idiot," Bridget said, but laughed and headed down after

her. She was more scientific about her descent, choosing a zigzagging path and keeping her weight against the mountain. A few minutes later, she waved from the bottom.

Olivia looked down the cliff nervously. "I'll stay here."

Polly didn't argue. She couldn't even look at Olivia, knowing the things that had been said about Baba in her house.

Polly headed down the cliff, hollering as she rode a wave of rocks, but somehow she made it to the bottom without killing herself. Close up, the river was a torrent even Bree might have liked, with slick, sharp rocks and whirlpool currents. Bridget surveyed the willows along the shore, while Mandy jumped sure-footedly from rock to rock. Her blue aura was exactly the color of the frigid stream, so it was a while before Polly realized Mandy had stepped right into the water. She knelt down and tickled her hand across the surface, then dipped deeper and came out with a nine-inch silver fish.

Bridget dropped the downed willow branches she'd collected. "No way!"

Mandy let the fish go as Polly and Bridget made their way to the water's edge. Dozens of silver fish battled the current and kept leaping toward the sky, as if mistaking Mandy's aura for deeper water.

"No one will believe this," Mandy said.

Polly touched her arm. "*I* believe it."

Bridget stared at the river, stunned but smiling. "Me too."

They were still smiling at one another when Polly saw the blue fabric. A jacket, or what remained of it, caught on a snag upstream.

"Oh," Mandy said as the fish darted away. "Oh no."

Polly glanced up the cliff, where Olivia still sat glumly on a rock. Polly could have said it was time to get back and no one would have argued, but instead she waded into the icy stream. Water quickly splashed over her knees as she battled the current and made it to the snag. Balancing on slick rocks and ignoring the cold, she struggled with fabric and limbs, but the jacket wouldn't budge. Mandy and Bridget stood on shore, watching her nervously as Polly grabbed the coat and gave it a vicious tug. There was a loud tear as she fell into the water, but when she got to her feet she held most of the jacket. Only an oddly delicate sleeve still dangled on a branch.

Tucking the tattered remains beneath her arm, Polly slowly made her way back to shore. Wet from the waist down and shivering, she hardly noticed her friends coming over to examine the coat and console her. She couldn't focus on anything except the tag, the one with letters written in permanent marker, in her sister's messy script: *Bree Greene.*

"Polly," Mandy said.

Polly gathered the coat against her chest and marched to the cliff. She didn't notice how long she climbed or how steep the slope; she was too busy convincing herself that the jacket's condition meant nothing. The wind could have carried it away, or Baba might have given Bree another coat weeks ago. Maybe she didn't even need a coat! If there was magic, then Bree could be warm all winter in nothing but a T-shirt and jeans.

At the top, Polly marched right past Olivia. Back in the grove, she threw the coat on the boulder and grabbed her bow and drill. Bridget had collected poplar branches, which Polly hated to burn. Her grandmother could have used the inner bark to make aspirin, but when Polly looked around there was nothing else. She worked the drill so intently, she hardly noticed when her friends came up behind her.

"Polly?" Bridget said, crouching beside her. "We should go. It's getting dark."

Polly ignored her as sparks began to fly. Once she had a good blaze, she took the jacket onto her soggy lap.

"Polly?" Olivia said. "Please, it's getting late."

"Bree doesn't need a jacket," Polly said. "Fairies don't wear coats."

She knew by their silence that they thought she'd gone right over the edge, but she no longer cared.

"Fairies don't need jackets," she said again. "They fall asleep in winter and return in spring."

Olivia put her hand on Polly's shoulder, but Polly jerked it off. She wasn't mad anymore, she just wanted them to go. Finally, Bridget asked if she'd be all right alone.

"I'll be fine," Polly said.

She waited until they left and their voices had faded away down the hill, then she examined the jacket more closely. A strand of blond hair had been snagged by the Velcro and the nylon pierced by thorns. But a watertight inner pocket was still zipped shut, and inside it Polly found a yellow lighter and an Altoids tin, empty except for the piece of parchment paper that had once covered the mints.

Polly tried to imagine what Bree had thought when she'd eaten her last Altoid and why she hadn't taken the lighter, but she wasn't going to draw any horrible conclusions. She stayed very still, like a rabbit in the brush when something big and scary walks by, her heart beating so quickly it hurt.

She fingered the parchment. She used to have paper like that, and a special pen. She'd write notes to the fairies and leave them on her windowsill, asking who their queen was and what they ate. Sometimes they answered instantly, other times it took a few days. Olivia had told her to compare the tiny writing to her mother's, but Polly never had. She had stopped writing rather than risk it. Again, it seemed best not to know anything for sure.

Now she reached into the fire and pulled out a black coal. She felt the sting of the heat but didn't flinch or cry out. She imagined her skin hardening like an eggshell, protecting all the soft, fragile stuff inside. She scraped the coal with her fingernail, carving it into a fine point.

The charcoal was her pencil, the parchment her fairy note. *Dear Bree,* she wrote. *Are you okay?*

But what if Bree didn't answer? What if it *had* been her mom pretending to be the fairy queen and replying to Polly's notes? What if Baba didn't know where Bree was, what if Bree was just a girl with a death wish, what if life was as merciless and magic-less as that?

Polly had cramps now, terrible ones just below her navel. She looked at the note in her hand, then tossed it into the flames. The moment it ignited, she threw in the jacket too. The coat melted rather than burned, sending up a cloud of foul-smelling smoke, and Polly smiled grimly. Without evidence to the contrary, Bree could still be out there. No one could say for sure that she was dead.

15

KINNIKINNICK

(Arctostaphylos)

The Greek name Arctostaphylos *means
"bear berries," while kinnikinnick is a Native
American word that translates as "smoking
mixture." The tart, mealy berries are invalu-
able, remaining edible throughout the coldest
part of the year. The plant helps alleviate in-
flammations of the urinary and digestive tracts.*

$\mathscr{P}$olly didn't tell her friends that she burned the jacket. In
fact, she asked them not to mention the discovery of Bree's
coat at all. Not only would it cause her parents more grief,
she explained, it might bring another posse to the woods, and
perhaps even lead to the discovery of Girlwood. It would do
nothing to help Bree.

So at lunch they talked of other things, of silver fish and
Bridget's wigwam, of a sheltered cave where the sweetroot was
still green. At one point they got so loud, John Bender leaned

over from the table he shared with Peter Wendell and asked if they'd become wilderness survivalists. The girls looked at one another, then Bridget said, "We're enjoying the woods while we still can."

"No kidding," John said. "I've been thinking about Mountain Winds ever since the debate. We've got to do something!"

The boys joined the girls' table. Peter had an uncle who worked for a state senator, and he said it wouldn't hurt to give him a call.

"We could circulate a petition," John said.

"And hand out flyers!" Bridget added. "This is great! We can't just sit here and let the Leylands ruin everything. I'll print up something tonight."

※ ※ ※ ※

In the cafeteria the next day, Bridget showed off a flyer with STOP MOUNTAIN WINDS printed in bold black ink. Everyone agreed it was perfect until Lily Bentz, a goth girl who rarely spoke to anyone, said it had no punch.

"Oh yeah?" Bridget said. "What do you suggest?"

Lily grabbed the flyer and quickly sketched a disturbing landscape of bare ravaged mountainsides, tombstones, and smoke—absolutely over the top, and a runaway hit. When John asked why Lily wasn't in his advanced art class, the goth girl actually blushed. Peter said he could make copies at his father's office. Suddenly they had a plan.

"We'll distribute these at school first," Bridget said. "Then go door to door. Maybe even to Carly's house."

Mandy giggled as she bit into an apple. She never ate sweets anymore, not even outside Girlwood. Then suddenly, she stopped laughing. Polly turned to find Carly right behind her, peering over her shoulder at the flyer.

Everyone around them had gone quiet. Then Carly waved her hand dismissively, as if they were too pathetic to be believed.

"Are you going to hang that on the refrigerator?" she asked. "Because Mountain Winds is a done deal. By next spring, you won't recognize the place."

She laughed as she walked away, and with a sinking heart Polly knew that she was right. The mountain had already been sacrificed and sold; builders and lawyers and even her own mother had seen to that. She looked around the table, knowing they were just fooling themselves, yet for some reason Olivia burst out laughing. Even more surprising, Lily grinned too. Then, as if someone had given the signal, the whole table erupted into hysterics. The lunch ladies paused with scoops of rice in their serving spoons.

Carly turned back. "Are you guys drunk or something?" she asked, which only made them laugh more.

"What a bunch of spazzes," Carly said.

As she walked away, Polly looked around the table. "Would someone please tell me what's so funny?"

That started another wave of hysterics. It was five minutes before anyone spoke.

"She started it," Mandy said at last, pointing to Olivia. "I saw her face and—"

"Yeah," Lily said. "It's her fault. I never laugh like that."

Everyone turned to Olivia. She and Polly hadn't spoken much since Polly found Bree's jacket, but now Olivia reached over and took her hand.

"I couldn't help it," Olivia said. "I wasn't sure about Gir— I mean, about the woods, but now I think we've got to fight for it, if only to wipe that smug look off Carly's face."

They all nodded, still giggly and happy, and Polly was horrified to realize she was the only one Facing Facts. She forced a smile, but she couldn't forget how that angelica had died before it even had a chance to save her grandmother, and how it had been Baba herself who told her there are some fights you just can't win.

❦ ❦ ❦ ❦

Polly circulated petitions and tried to be hopeful, but even the weather seemed to be on the Leylands' side. A week before Christmas break, exactly eighty days after Bree had disappeared, Laramie got one of those fluky winter warm spells: T-shirt weather in December and perfect conditions for bull-dozers. Even when she went into her bedroom and closed the window, Polly heard the rumble of machinery. Every time a picture rattled on the wall, she knew another tree came down.

Yet the mixed-up seasons had done some good. The chick-weed started growing again, and, most important, Baba's health improved. The warm sun drew her out to the garden, where Polly could barely make out her rainbow in the dry air.

The last day of school before the Christmas holiday could have passed for spring, and that afternoon Polly and the girls hiked to Girlwood in short sleeves. Mandy caught two fish, and they grilled them over the fire. With a topping of bear-berries, which stay edible all winter, they sat down to a feast.

While Mandy doled out pieces of the flaky white trout, Polly went to gather more wood. Loaded up with fallen larch branches, she didn't see the wolves until she was nearly back to the fire.

It appeared to be the same wolf pack as before, led by the black male and the tan female with the gash on her snout. Polly counted eight of them, including one that looked like Bronco, even though he didn't wag his tail or bark. He stopped on some silent command from his leader, ears pricked, tail down, fully transformed.

Mandy, Bridget, and Olivia went on talking, oblivious to the danger creeping in around them. Polly stepped forward, and the leader growled from deep in his throat. The girls stopped talking abruptly, and Mandy's face went pale.

Polly clutched the branches against her chest. "Get into the shelter," she whispered. "Don't run, or they'll chase you."

For a moment, none of them moved, then Bridget slowly got to her feet. The black wolf had a terrifying flaming aura. He was the vicious one, Polly knew, the one to fear. Bridget helped Mandy to her feet, then glanced across the fire at Olivia, who just sat there, mesmerized.

"Go," Polly said.

With one more glance at Olivia, Bridget and Mandy slowly backed into the lean-to. The black wolf bared his teeth.

"Oh my God." Mandy's voice came from the shelter. "Did you see . . ."

"Sssssh."

Polly knelt down to drop the wood, and the female's ears pricked up. Olivia still hadn't budged. Polly swallowed hard and inched forward, trying not to make any sudden movements. At any moment, the wolves could spring, yet Olivia seemed clueless, smiling as Polly approached.

"Wolves!" she said, her eyes wide.

"No kidding," Polly whispered, grabbing Olivia's arm. "Come on."

Olivia kept twisting and turning. "Is it the same pack?" she asked, not bothering to whisper. "Could that be Bronco? I count eight. How many do you see?"

Polly wanted to strangle her, but she focused on leading Olivia past the last wolf. An unusual rust color and well over a hundred pounds, the animal stood between them and the lean-to, his body low and ready to pounce.

When the fur stood up on the back of the wolf's neck, even Olivia went silent.

"Just walk past it slowly," Polly whispered. "Pretend you're not afraid."

Olivia nodded, though Polly could feel her shaking. Polly nudged her forward, and the wolf crouched lower. Then he sprang.

Polly cried out at the brush of thick fluffy fur against her arm, but the wolf was merely racing past them toward the fire. The leader pair tore into the fish, and while the others waited deferentially for scraps, Polly pushed Olivia into the shelter and fell in after her, her legs weak with terror and relief.

When the food was gone, the female raised her head and looked toward the girls.

Polly tried to keep Olivia back, but she acted like she'd just seen a movie star and wanted a better view. The female stepped forward, low to the ground, and bared her teeth. Polly couldn't believe this was happening—she'd been certain nothing could hurt them in Girlwood.

"Get back," Polly said, but Olivia did just the opposite and stepped out of the shelter.

Olivia and the female faced each other, then something deep and strange rose from Olivia's throat. The wolf tilted her head as if the guttural sound painted a picture in her mind of a wolf in girl's clothing, an ally where an enemy ought to be.

Polly's skin prickled. "Olivia, please!" she whispered.

She should never have spoken. The moment the words left her lips, the black wolf attacked. He charged the shelter, fangs bared, the light around him blazing. Polly barely had time to snatch Olivia back before the female jumped between them. Olivia cried out as the two wolves tore into each other. Everything happened so fast, Polly couldn't make sense of it. The wolves were snarling, then from the entrance to the grove came shouting, footsteps, a gunshot. Something whimpered.

"No!" Olivia screamed.

Olivia rushed forward, but the female was already down. The other wolves and Bronco scattered as Polly's mother and grandmother ran into the grove. Officer Wendt stood over the wolf, aiming his gun at the animal's head to shoot again.

"No!" Olivia cried, throwing herself on the wolf.

"Get away from it!" the officer shouted.

The wolf might have taken Olivia for a kindred spirit, but the animal was wounded now, in a panic to escape. She writhed on the ground, teeth bared and her lethal claws flailing at Olivia's jeans. For a moment, Polly thought the wolf hadn't broken the skin because Olivia didn't cry out. But as Olivia stood, Polly saw the tear in the fabric and the blood seeping through.

In the fading light, Olivia's eyes were watery with pain. "I can't believe you shot her. She saved us."

Officer Wendt lowered his gun. Baba hung back, her medicine bag slung around her neck, the rainbow around her strong again. Polly's mom's face was ashen, but she was the only one who didn't just stand there. She pushed past Officer Wendt and pulled Olivia from the wolf.

"No!" Olivia said again, squirming. "Don't kill her!"

Polly's mother gripped Olivia's arm and looked at her like she was crazy. "Those wolves were going to kill you!" She turned to Polly. "I got off work early and went to Olivia's to pick you up. Her mother had no idea where you were. Then when we tried Bridget's and Mandy's houses, no one could find any of you!"

Olivia was hysterical, writhing as much as the wolf. They seemed to move in unison, even their bleeding matched drop for drop.

Baba stepped forward. "I think you'd better leave that wolf alone," she said to the policeman. "These girls are upset enough. They don't need you to kill a poor creature right in front of them."

"It's a *wolf*," the man said. "A goddamn nuisance animal."

Baba stared at him, and even though he was a large man with a gun in his hand, he somehow looked like the one in danger.

"You've done enough," Baba said quietly. "She's already dying."

Olivia buried her face in her hands as Polly's mom confronted Bridget and Mandy. "Do you realize what could have happened if my mother hadn't figured out where you were? You could all be dead right now! Your parents are out of their minds with worry. Do you think this is a joke? Making up phony choirs and chess clubs? Lying?"

She cast a white, cold light, and none of the girls spoke. "I had to call the police. *Again*," Polly's mother went on. "You should have seen your parents' faces when they found out all of you were missing. They thought they might end up like me."

None of them dared to look up as Olivia's weeping filled the air. Polly felt sick inside, not only at the sight of the dying wolf, but because she knew the magic was over. The secret of Girlwood was out.

"How could you do this to me, Polly?" her mother asked, her voice breaking.

Polly could think of nothing to say as the wolf's eyes rolled back in her head.

"We've got to save her," Olivia said, turning toward Baba.

"If the bullet went through cleanly," Baba said, "there might be something I can do."

"Oh no, there isn't," Officer Wendt insisted. They had almost forgotten about him, but now he stepped forward, towering over them all. "This is my jurisdiction and there's no way you're going to—"

Baba walked past him. Polly wondered if the man also saw her grandmother's rainbow, because he raised his hand to shield his eyes. By the time he dropped it, Baba had already crouched beside the wolf. The animal was too weak to bite now. There was a rainbow around them both.

Baba slid her medicine bag off her neck. "I'll need water," she said to Mandy. "It's getting dark. Can you still make it to the river?"

Mandy was already moving toward the cliff. Officer Wendt reached out to grab her, but she slipped past, as slippery as a fish.

"Come back here!" the policeman shouted. "Young lady, do you hear me?" Mandy had already disappeared through the trees. "Is anyone listening to me?"

Baba took something from her bag, and the wolf's nose twitched as she slipped whatever it was into the animal's mouth. "She should go to sleep soon."

Olivia and Bridget edged closer to the wolf, but when Polly tried to move forward, her mother grabbed her arm.

"Oh no," her mom said. "You're not going anywhere near that thing."

Polly wrenched her arm free. "I want to help Baba."

"No," her mother said. "This isn't your decision."

But Polly thought that it was. In Girlwood, things weren't necessarily easier, but it was always clear what had to be done. Polly crossed the grove to take her place beside her grandmother—the one spot that had always comforted her, but that now, as her mother began to cry, felt like a million miles from home.

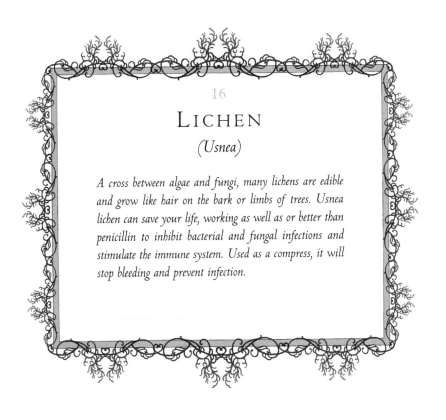

16

LICHEN
(Usnea)

A cross between algae and fungi, many lichens are edible and grow like hair on the bark or limbs of trees. Usnea lichen can save your life, working as well as or better than penicillin to inhibit bacterial and fungal infections and stimulate the immune system. Used as a compress, it will stop bleeding and prevent infection.

Polly's mom ran after her but drew back when the wolf snarled.

"Please step away from it, Polly," she pleaded.

But Polly had made her choice. Maybe she couldn't save everything, but that didn't mean she shouldn't try. "Why won't you ever believe things will turn out okay?" she said.

Her mom's gaze went past her in horror as Olivia crouched beside the wolf. The animal began to whimper, raising goose flesh on Polly's arms. She didn't care what anybody said: from that moment on, the female was Olivia's wolf, and Olivia was the wolf's girl.

Mandy ran back, carrying her tennis shoes. Water sloshed over the rims.

"I didn't have to go all the way to the stream," she said. "There's a spring about fifty yards in."

"All right," Officer Wendt said, squaring his shoulders. "We're done here. I'm taking you all home."

"No!" the girls cried in unison.

He ignored them and tried his radio, and then his cell phone. As he struggled to get reception, Baba thanked Mandy for the water and poured it over the wolf's wound. The animal thrashed her legs, but with Olivia there, she didn't attempt a getaway. Baba glanced at Olivia's torn jeans, but Olivia shook her head.

"It doesn't hurt much," she said. "We've got to save her."

"We're not saving anything," Polly's mom interrupted. "We're taking you home so your parents can have some peace."

Her voice was so unyielding, even Bree might not have argued. The wolf was getting sleepy, her eyelids beginning to flutter.

"Valerian and willow bark," Baba said, smiling. "Works every time." She touched the wolf's head gently, and the animal closed her eyes. "Once she's asleep, I'll see what I can do about that wound. Looks like the bullet went through cleanly. If I sew it up, she might have a chance."

Officer Wendt slammed his cell phone shut, unable to find a signal. "We'd better head down," he said, looking at Baba, who gently probed the wolf's wound.

"The girls know the way," Baba told him. "You can't expect me to leave her."

Polly knew that was exactly what he expected, but it was her mother who spoke. "The girls are *twelve*," she said, as if that meant they weren't capable of anything. Even the larches seemed offended, no longer leaning in to listen. The hushed, charged air of Girlwood disappeared. "We need to leave before the other wolves come back," her mom went on. "Even you must see that."

Baba looked up. "All I see is that if I take you home, this wolf might die before I get back."

Officer Wendt put his gun in his holster. "We can only hope," he said.

🐾 🐾 🐾 🐾

Baba reluctantly left the wolf sleeping and guided them back through the woods. "That animal's life is on your shoulders, Faith," she said as they neared the town.

Back in cell phone range, Officer Wendt called Mandy's and Bridget's parents and gave them the news that their daughters were all right.

"I'll have them home in fifteen minutes," he said, then hung up and asked for Olivia's number.

Olivia whirled to face him. "I can't believe you made us leave her!" she said, a golden-tipped light standing up on the back of her neck.

"The wolf?" Officer Wendt said. "Are you crazy? You'll likely need a rabies shot."

When Olivia merely glared at him, Polly's mom grabbed the phone. "I know her number," she said. She gave him back the phone just as Mrs. Nelson answered.

"Everything's fine," Officer Wendt said. "I've found the girls." Ignoring Olivia's furious gaze, he went on painting himself as a wolf-killing hero and said he and the girls were on their way to Baba's house right now. It was only when he paused for commendations that he noticed Mrs. Nelson had begun to shout.

The policeman's smile faltered. "I don't see how . . ." He held the phone away from his ear, then brought it back cautiously. "But that's ridiculous. She's the one who led us . . . Fine. You can meet us there."

He snapped the phone shut and jammed it in his pocket. "I'll walk Bridget and Mandy home. Olivia," he said, looking sympathetic for the first time all day, "your mom wants to pick you up."

❦ ❦ ❦ ❦

Mrs. Nelson must have run every stoplight in town, because she was waiting outside Baba's garden when the group emerged from the woods. Officer Wendt didn't even look at her. He lugged Mandy and Bridget down the street, giving them no chance to say goodbye.

Olivia stood nervously by the purple ash as Baba tiredly crossed the yard. "How nice of you to come all the way out here to collect Olivia," Baba said.

Mrs. Nelson flinched, as if Baba's breath were laced with arsenic. She usually wore her hair up in a neat ponytail, but tonight the dark strands hung in her eyes, and her sweater was on inside out. She waited until Baba had gone in the house, then called to Olivia, "Get in the car. We're going."

At the sound of her mother's voice, Olivia glanced back at the woods.

"Olivia!" Mrs. Nelson said again. She threw open the gate despite its BEWARE sign and strode across the garden. "Do you hear me?"

Polly wanted to say that everyone on the block could hear her, but her mother narrowed her eyes in warning.

Mrs. Nelson's gaze fell to Olivia's ripped jeans. "Oh my God. Is that blood? What have they done to you?"

Polly couldn't believe it, but Olivia didn't cry. Even when her mother pulled back the torn fabric and poked her, Olivia had the pride and restraint of a wolf.

Mrs. Nelson took her by the shoulders. "Answer me!"

"She tried to save a wolf!" Polly shouted. "It was the bravest thing I've ever seen."

Carly Leyland had given Polly a fair number of sneers, but nothing could have prepared her for the look of revulsion on Mrs. Nelson's face. It was like Polly had brought in some dreadful pestilence—a plague or a swarm of killer bees.

"I should never have allowed this friendship," the woman said, looking nervously around the yard as if the plants might jump up and grab her. "Pastor Bentley warned me, but I didn't want to make judgments. This is all my fault. Who knows what you've done to her, the things you've made her do."

"I didn't make her do anything," Polly said, her hands in fists.

"No? Then you used some kind of black magic on her. She's a *good* girl. She goes to church and studies hard and loves her family. Can you stand there and tell me this wasn't all your idea? Luring Olivia out to the middle of nowhere? Putting her life in jeopardy and convincing her to lie?"

Polly stepped back. Everything Olivia's mom said was right, but it was wrong, too. It *had* been Polly's idea, but Olivia belonged in Girlwood as much as the rest of them. She was more than just good. She was brave and loyal and willing to sacrifice herself for someone else—she was the wolf's girl.

"Carol," Polly's mom said, "let's calm down. The girls made a terrible mistake, but I think—"

"Don't tell me to calm down! This goes beyond lying and sneaking around. It's wickedness. You know it is. What have they been doing out there? Ask yourself that. I'm sorry for your loss, Faith, but frankly I can't believe you'd let another one of your daughters run loose. It's like you want to be rid of them both."

Olivia finally sprang to life. "How can you say that? It practically killed her when Bree disappeared."

The light around Polly's mom flickered and grew dim. It was only then that Polly realized it had been turning yellow, like a slow-healing bruise. Her mother *had* been getting better, whether she wanted to or not. It might have seemed like the world should stop after Bree disappeared, but it hadn't. And, more than that, Polly's mom was Baba's daughter, too strong to simply curl up and die.

Polly leaned against her mother. Her power, she realized, wasn't only in Girlwood, in a bow and drill, but in something far simpler: in a promise to her mother that she wouldn't leave her too. She could be the daughter her mother needed, the only one she had left. As she turned her face into her mom's shoulder, a little "oh" escaped Faith Greene's lips. She lowered her face to Polly's wild hair.

"If you're lost in the woods, even in winter, you know the one plant that can sustain you?" Baba asked. She'd come out of the house so silently, Mrs. Nelson squealed and put a hand to her throat.

"Lichen," Polly said, pressing her head to her mother's chest.

Baba nodded in satisfaction. "Exactly. Why?"

"Because it grows all year," Polly told her. "And some types, like usnea, can save your life by fighting infections."

"Yes!" Baba said, showing off a handful of the stringy gray-green lichen, then tucking it into the medicine bag around her neck. "Usnea can actually shrink tumors. Out in the woods, you can apply it directly to an open wound." She smiled at Olivia's mother, who stared back with alarm.

"We're going, Olivia," Mrs. Nelson said.

"But I want to go with them!" Olivia cried. "The wolf needs me!"

Mrs. Nelson looked like she was about to have a heart attack. "We're going straight to Pastor Bentley's house," she said, dragging Olivia to the car. "He'll know what to do."

Polly tried to go after them, but Mrs. Nelson locked the car doors. As she screeched out of the driveway, Polly couldn't help but wonder if Olivia's mother was right. Maybe they *were* wicked. Wicked because they loved nature more than church; because they thought light and beauty were just as likely to be found in a wolf or Baba's amazing herbs as in people; because they didn't think someone like Pastor Bentley should get to decide what was holy or good.

Maybe they were wicked, but if so, she was glad.

Baba stepped up beside them, the rainbow around her enveloping them all. "Nice lady," Baba said. "We should have her over more often."

Polly was stunned when her mother and grandmother laughed at the same moment. It was eerie, like beautiful, forbidden music.

"You look tired, Mom," Polly's mom said.

Baba waved her off. "I'm fine. I've got to get up to that wolf, though."

Baba had walked a thousand miles, yet Polly doubted that she could make it one more. It was enough to make her cry, but instead Polly squared her shoulders. Lichen, she thought, to prevent infection. Goldenrod to stop the bleeding. A needle and thread. She could save that wolf herself. She'd watch the animal's aura to see if she was recovering or fading. Polly would never be her grandmother, but she would have to do.

She only had to convince her mother, but Faith Greene was

now staring wide-eyed at the rainbow that stretched from Baba's head to the treetops. She said nothing, but Polly would have bet a million dollars that she saw it—something a logical person would have sworn couldn't be there.

"You don't have to go, Baba," Polly said. "I can do it."

All of them froze. As Polly's mother dropped her gaze from Baba's rainbow, Polly's heart fluttered like a bird in her chest. Her mom studied her long and hard, until, with a sigh, she finally nodded.

"We'll go together," she said. "You can stay here this time, Mom."

Baba's shoulders sagged in relief, as if some words had the same soothing properties as chickweed. She lifted her medicine bag off her neck and handed it to Polly.

"Oh," Polly said, feeling like there were feathers inside her, lifting her off the ground.

Baba turned to Polly's mom and smiled. "Thank you, Faith," she said.

❧ ❧ ❧ ❧

They found the wolf still sleeping, the golden light around her dim.

Polly gritted her teeth as she used goldenrod to stop the bleeding, then packed the wound with lichen to keep infection at bay. She pretended the skin was merely fabric as she stitched it closed. She couldn't see pain the way Baba could, but she had her own guide—the light around the wolf that brightened slightly as she worked.

"Baba couldn't have done it better," her mother said as Polly bit off the end of the thread. Polly's hands trembled once it was over. She swore if she looked in the mirror, she would see a different person. An older one, hardly a girl at all.

"Now we wait," her mom went on, "and hope she wakes up."

For two hours, it looked like she wouldn't. The wolf lay so still Polly had to press her ear to the animal's chest to hear a heartbeat. Then, at last, the leader opened her eyes. She snarled and struggled, and Polly and her mother leaped to their feet. Still too weak to stand, though, the wolf merely looked from face to face, searching.

"She wants Olivia," Polly said, and lowered her head. So did she.

17

OXEYE DAISY
(Chrysanthemum leucanthemum)

Though many consider it a weed, the ancient Greeks dedicated the oxeye daisy to Artemis, the virgin huntress, and Christians to Mary Magdalene, both believing it a powerful herb for women. The leaves are edible, with a taste and texture like romaine lettuce, and the flowers contain compounds useful in making safe, natural insecticides.

$\mathcal{I}$t was after midnight when Polly and her mother finally left the wolf and walked home.

"Thank God you're all right!" Polly's dad said, hurrying down the porch steps. "I drove over here hours ago. Max Wendt came to the cabin to tell me what happened."

Polly's mom motioned for Polly to go inside. "Get in your pajamas, honey," she said. "I need to talk to your dad."

Polly was too tired to argue, but when she got inside she

paused at the top of the stairs. Her parents' voices were muted at first, then slowly grew more intense. Polly crouched in the shadows when they came inside.

". . . looked terrible," her mother was saying. "Feeble, Paul."

"I can't believe how close those girls came to disaster."

They stepped into the living room, out of view. "She handed over her medicine bag like she was passing the torch to Polly," her mom went on. "It's just like my mother, isn't it? She does everything she can to make me hate her, then starts dying to trip me up."

"I doubt she's doing that on purpose, Faith."

"Oh no? How many people do I have to lose? What did I do to make Bree leave? What if I do the same thing to Polly?"

"It wasn't your fault. Bree—"

Her dad's voice broke, and Polly knelt on the landing.

"Bree had to go," her dad continued. "We may never know why, but she had to. That's the only way I can bear to think of it. As for Polly, just don't try to tame her, Faith. You may not want to hear this, but she's a lot like your mother. "

Polly straightened her spine, a tingle creeping up her fingers toward her wrists. As each hair on her arm rose, a tendril of green light spiraled up after it, bathing the landing in a soothing emerald glow.

"How did you go on?" her mom asked. "Answer me that, Paul. After Bree, how can anything still matter?"

Polly closed her eyes and counted to ten. Even before she opened them again, she knew the green glow had faded. She felt her skin cooling, and when she finally looked around the landing, she saw only normal things—a warm brown floor, a white-painted table, a blue vase.

Downstairs, her dad shushed her mother, saying things he hadn't in years. Why, Polly wondered, didn't he talk like this all the time? Why was it only grief that inspired him?

"We can't give up," he said. "Every day is another chance for her to come back. We've got to believe that, Faith."

"I've been leaving things," her mom told him. "Food, clothes."

"I know. Polly told me. I've been cutting firewood and stacking it in the woods." He sounded ashamed, like he'd made a fool of himself.

"Eighty-seven days," her mom said.

All of a sudden, Polly had to remind herself of Bree's last words. Had she said she'd be all right, or had Polly just imagined that part? Even if Bree had gone into the woods, even if they left her everything she needed, there were a million ways not to survive. That's what Bree was really good at—finding the sinkhole in otherwise solid ground. Turning food into a weapon, her home into a prison, friends into spies and thieves. She could easily make a place as magical and bountiful as Girlwood a grave.

Polly fought her tears but began to tremble. Eighty-seven days. A miraculous amount of time for a girl to survive alone in the wilderness.

"Faith," her dad said. "Faith."

Polly heard their footsteps down the hall and her mother's bedroom door open, then close. It felt peculiar to be still listening, so she went into her room and turned on the radio to help her sleep.

❧ ❧ ❧ ❧

In the morning, her father was in the kitchen making pancakes. He smiled too brightly, like an actor in a commercial hawking Aunt Jemima. Her mother jumped up from the table, playing his hungry, happy wife.

"Your mom and I have wonderful news," he said. "So much has happened, but last night we talked. We've decided to try again."

Polly closed her eyes for a moment to take it all in, but when she opened them again, her elation waned. Her mom was smiling, but the light around her had a pinkish tinge.

"Really?" Polly said.

Her mom laughed. "Yes, really. Aren't you happy?"

Polly wanted to ask her the same thing, but she didn't dare. Instead, she rushed to hug them both, praying that happiness simply grew more complicated as you got older, and sometimes, if it had to, even started with a lie.

🌿 🌿 🌿 🌿

Christmas came; then Polly's thirteenth birthday, which passed without a party because Olivia's mom wouldn't let her come; then the snow. When it was a foot deep, construction on Mountain Winds was officially halted until spring. Polly was grateful for the temporary reprieve, but the sudden silence also made her realize that winter was no longer a threat, it was an actuality. It took every bit of her imagination to picture Bree curled up in that abandoned cabin, feasting on green vegetables and burning their dad's firewood until spring.

Polly's mother made her promise that she would no longer sneak off to Girlwood, and Polly kept her word. From her bedroom window, she watched the snow grow so thick, nothing moved except the wolves. Polly spotted them one evening, the female they'd saved standing just beyond the trees and howling as if the pack was one wolf short. But when Polly opened her window, the animals scattered, the female limping only slightly as she dashed into the brush. Polly waited night after night, even howling herself one time to try to entice them, but she never saw them again.

Winter seemed the time to move on. Polly's dad closed up the cabin and came back home, once again doing the dishes and shoveling the driveway while Polly's mom planted a smile on her face and ignored the sawdust he tracked in from the garage. Though Polly listened for signs of strain, what she heard instead was eerie politeness—*pleases* and *thank yous* that, for some reason, made her hold her breath. Every time her parents prattled on about house repairs and the weather, Polly wondered what they really wanted to talk about. What would happen when all their dull conversations dried up?

School, surprisingly, became Polly's refuge. There, she could breathe right and, most importantly, see Olivia.

"Can you believe that test?" Olivia asked after the last bell on Monday. While most of the kids bolted for the exits, they lingered by their lockers. Olivia's mom would be waiting outside.

"It was totally impossible," Polly said.

"And what about that drama at lunch?"

Polly rolled her eyes. Carly Leyland and Crystal had been going at it in the cafeteria. Polly had no idea what had caused the rift, but Carly hadn't been satisfied until Crystal cried.

"Poor Crystal," Olivia said.

"Crystal needs to pick better friends," Polly told her.

Familiar laughter spilled down the stairwell. "Speaking of the devil," Polly said.

Crystal must have groveled her way back into Carly's good graces because they came down the stairs together, all smiles. Joy was there too, to complete the trifecta—girls one, two, and three in their designer jeans and boyfriends' football jerseys. Carly still wore Joe Meyer's number 24.

Carly caught a glimpse of Olivia's rumpled beige coat. "Nice jacket, *Liv*," she said. "Are you joining the army?"

Joy and Crystal thought that was hysterical, and Carly turned her attention to Polly's orange windbreaker. "Is it hunting season already? Be careful what you shoot. I hear there are wolf girls running loose."

Olivia stepped forward suddenly. "What's wrong with you?" she asked, loudly enough to stop conversation in the hall.

All eyes turned toward Carly, and for a moment, Polly would have sworn she was looking at Bree. At a girl who asked herself that very question a hundred times a day. *What's wrong with you? What's wrong with you?* Then Carly narrowed her eyes.

"*You* are, Wolf Girl," she said, laughing as she towed Joy and Crystal away.

Polly touched Olivia's arm. "Yeah, that's the girl you want for your friend," she said. "Great judge of character, *Liv*."

Olivia shoved her and they laughed until Olivia's mom pulled up in the drop-off lane. After Olivia had gone, Polly wandered through the hall, not ready to face her father's polite questions about her day or the sight of him wandering aimlessly from room to room. She was still at her locker ten minutes later when Bridget and Mandy came looking for her.

"There you are!" Bridget said.

Their brush with wolves and the wrath of their parents hadn't curbed their devotion to Girlwood. Bridget had been grounded for two weeks, but at school she'd formed a club called Kids for the Woods. Polly, Mandy, and Olivia were her first members, but within days, she had a dozen more. Lily and some of her goth friends showed up at lunch, along with John and Peter. The day they made the news for cleaning up a portion of Sheep Creek, twenty-six new students had crammed into the library. Even Crystal came, though she kept looking over her shoulder to make sure Carly didn't catch her there.

"We want you to see something," Bridget said. She unzipped her backpack, revealing a mound of small, dark green leaves. "My family went on vacation to Nevada last weekend, and when I went on a hike I found these."

Polly lifted out a few of the leaves and sniffed them. "Oxeye daisies," she said.

Bridget turned to Mandy. "See? I told you that's what they were." She smiled proudly. "I had my field guide with me."

"I can't believe you found so much," Polly said.

"It's summer all year there, as far as I can tell. Anyway,

we've got snowshoes. We're going to leave these for Bree."

Polly didn't know what to say. She hadn't thought that any of them would go back. Ever. She'd thought it was done.

"I . . . I promised my mom I wouldn't go," Polly said.

Mandy touched her arm. "We know the way. We'll take care of her, Polly. It's not only you anymore."

Polly blinked back tears, both in gratitude and horrible, horrible doubt. Could a few wild greens really sustain a girl through winter? Could Bree, or anyone, change that much, from victim to survivor, wraith to fairy, just like that? It was a lovely notion, but now Polly saw that it was also ridiculous— the fanciful visions of girls.

Yet her friends were smiling, bright-eyed, and hopeful. She felt protective of their optimism, the way a mother would feel if she found a note her daughter had written to the fairies and would do anything to keep that kind of innocence alive.

"Bree will love that," Polly managed to say. "Thanks."

❧ ❧ ❧ ❧

Polly's dad picked her up from school. The truck cab was sparkling, not a wood shaving in sight.

"How was your day?" he asked.

Usually she said "Fine," whether it was true or not, but today something in his tense manner kept her silent. A few days ago, her mother had brought up the idea of his going back to the law firm, and since then he hadn't touched a log in the garage. He hadn't trimmed his beard either, and it was looking a little wild.

"Polly," he said as he pulled away from the curb. She wanted him to call her his lovely fairy Gwendolyn, but she knew he wasn't going to. Just like her mother wanted them to be the Family That Had Moved On, but that hadn't happened either.

"I don't know how to say this," he said, and ran a hand through his hair. "The last thing your mother and I wanted was to disappoint you again . . ."

He popped the clutch on the truck and had to restart the engine. Even then, he only went a block, then he pulled to the curb. He kept his hands on the wheel, waiting for her to say something, but all Polly could think of was that she wished she were more surprised. She wished they could love each other simply because they'd lost the same thing.

"It's all right," Polly said. "You should go back to your cabin." She didn't know where the words came from. Her voice didn't sound like her own, but like some wise, hardened city girl's, a teenager who had seen it all.

He was the one who cried. "I'm so sorry, honey. I—"

"It'll be better for Mom," she said quickly, cutting him off. "You just remind her of everything. And I'm thirteen now. I'll be fine."

When he took her in his arms, she wanted to retract every word. In her head, she was screaming at him to stay, no matter what it cost him, but the words never left her lips.

"I love you, Polly," he said. "My fairy girl."

❧ ❧ ❧ ❧

They stopped for ice cream and took nearly an hour to eat double scoops. When they got home, she saw that he'd already packed. It had all been worked out. Her mother would be home early so she and Polly could talk.

"You be good to her, all right?" her dad said, and she stiffened. That's all she'd been lately: good. Going to school, coming straight home, giving up Olivia (for the most part), giving up Girlwood. Giving up on Bree.

He put his hands on her shoulders. "You're all your mother has now," he said.

Polly blinked in surprise. He was *wrong*. Her mother had plenty, if she'd only look past Bree's empty room. And Polly had plenty too. She had her friends and Baba and more belief than doubt. Maybe that wasn't the perfect world she used to create with her sister in the woods, but for real life, it was pretty good.

"That's too much to ask," she told him, "to be someone's whole world."

"But, Polly—"

"No," she said. "I'm not everything. I'm just me."

After he left, Polly went into the kitchen and grabbed the notepad from the drawer. With each stroke of the pen, she realized that, like it or not, she was no princess in need of saving. She would rather be the knight.

I'm going to the grove. I'm not giving up on her.
Polly

She grabbed her jacket and went out. Without snowshoes, she sank to her knees with each step, but she didn't turn back. By the time she slogged to the wall of devil's club, the afternoon light was fading, and her pants were soaked through.

Bridget and Mandy had had to dig away two feet of snow to reach the tunnel, making the entrance obvious. Polly dropped to the ground and slithered into the opening. Halfway through, she knew something was terribly wrong.

She couldn't hear the wind over the sound of voices. There was a party in Girlwood. As she came to her feet, she saw a roaring bonfire and a full keg of beer. She even thought she spotted Mandy and Bridget, but then a crowd moved between them. An older dark-haired boy thumped the keg, another threw lighter fluid onto the logs and cheered when the flames leaped skyward. They looked like high school seniors, older boys who wore only jeans and cotton shirts despite the cold.

She recognized a couple of girls from Bree's high school—Cathy Davidson in a neon pink jacket and Nan Tucker in her faux-fur boots and hat.

"What's going on?" Polly asked.

Still in Joe Meyer's football jersey, Carly Leyland leaned against Baba's tree to keep from falling down drunk. She held up her red plastic cup in greeting. "S-swamp Girl's here! Everybody? Say hello to Swam' Girl." Carly stumbled and broke a branch off Baba's tree. Polly saw Bridget pushing her way through the crowd.

"Swamp Girl, guess what?" Carly went on. "We're here to christen the place. My dad's going to put the community pool right here. Isn't that great? Who needs a fire pit when you've got a hot tub? We'll make these trees into deck chairs!"

She might have been drunk, but when she flung her cup at the larch, she hit it squarely. From the corner of her eye, Polly noticed Bridget reaching out for her, but by then it was too late. Polly was already charging. She was done being good.

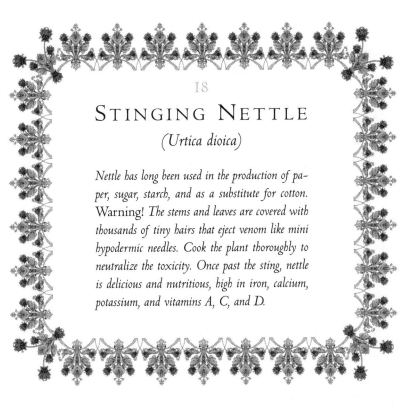

18

STINGING NETTLE

(*Urtica dioica*)

Nettle has long been used in the production of paper, sugar, starch, and as a substitute for cotton. Warning! *The stems and leaves are covered with thousands of tiny hairs that eject venom like mini hypodermic needles. Cook the plant thoroughly to neutralize the toxicity. Once past the sting, nettle is delicious and nutritious, high in iron, calcium, potassium, and vitamins A, C, and D.*

$\mathscr{B}$ridget caught up to her. "Polly," she said. "Listen."

Polly's ears were ringing. She'd just spotted Mandy holding a red plastic cup while the girls around her flung their beers at the trees.

"They just showed up," Bridget said. "I guess this place was no secret after what happened with the wolves. They must have followed our tracks."

It was amazing how much stuff they'd lugged up here—

not only a beer keg and plastic cups, but a stereo, CDs, even a few plastic chairs. But none of that bothered Polly as much as the sight of Carly aiming a second cup at Baba's tree.

Polly darted around Bridget and slapped the cup out of Carly's hand. For a moment, Polly thought Carly was too drunk to fight back, then she felt a painful jab in her knee.

Carly narrowed her eyes and kicked her again. "This isn't your party, Swamp Girl. We're celebrating our new pool. My dad said he might even put in a water slide."

Polly clutched her knee while everyone looked at her as if she were crazy. Only Swamp Girl would choose a few dumb trees over a water slide. Crystal and Joy showed the others where the pool would go, and when even Bridget and Mandy couldn't hide their interest, Polly's heart sank. If the girls of Girlwood didn't understand, there was no way anyone else would either. It wasn't just a few dumb trees; it was a refuge. An enchanted forest. Cut down the trees, and Bree would never come back.

"I want you out," Polly said, her voice echoing through the grove. Someone had turned off the radio. Conversations about the pool tapered off.

"Is that so?" Carly said. "We're supposed to take orders from Swamp Girl now? These aren't your woods, you know. They're mine. They belong to my father."

She pulled back her foot and Polly braced herself, but Carly merely kicked snow at her feet. With a nasty smile, she did it again. The high-schoolers laughed, and it took only a moment for Polly to recognize the remaining members of Bree's Fab Five.

Polly kicked the snow off her shoes. Her knee hurt but, strangely, not as much as the rest of her. She had shooting pains in her shoulders, a throbbing ache in her temples and in the small of her back.

"The woods don't belong to anyone," she said.

Carly smirked. "Oh yeah?"

Carly stroked the bark of the nearest tree. "Then why is this little gem going to be my coffee table next year?" She tapped another larch, wrinkling her nose. "This one looks too rotten to be anything but pulp."

Polly's eyes burned with unshed tears. Baba had always told her that you didn't have to like everyone, just as they didn't have to like you, but every creature deserved respect. Bree used to call statements like that Babaisms and said that they were total bullshit. Some people are slime, Bree had said, and can't be trusted. They'll hurt you the first chance they get.

Polly grabbed Baba's tree for support and pressed her cheek against the bark.

Carly laughed out loud. "What are you doing, Swamp Girl?" she asked. "Talking to the trees?"

Joe Meyer stepped from the crowd, wearing only jeans and a polo shirt. Like the other boys, he was pretending he wasn't cold even though his teeth were chattering.

"L-let's go, Carly," he said.

Carly ignored him. "Hello?" she said, and banged her fist against the larch she'd slated for pulp. "Mr. Tree? Anybody home?"

She kept rapping on the trunk so hard she should have gotten splinters.

"Swamp Girl," she said, "it's not answering. How rude."

The girls who'd been drinking straight from the beer keg found that hysterical, and found their own trunks to pound. Polly felt dizzy, as if the thumping were coming from inside her own chest.

"Kn-knock it off," Joe said, but none of the girls listened. Carly raised her fist to thwack another trunk, but at the last minute dropped her hand.

"Did you see that?" she said, glancing over her shoulder. "That tree just . . ."

She shook her head and stepped away from the larch. Polly stared at the weathered trunk and saw nothing out of the ordinary, yet Carly had gone pale.

"The loser woods," Carly said shakily. "That's what we should call it." She looked warily around the grove as if she were seeing ghosts instead of tree trunks, a face where a gnarled old knot ought to be.

"This is so lame," Carly continued. "Let's go to my house. It's warm inside and my parents are out for the night."

After some discussion, everyone agreed to move the party to Carly's. Someone folded up the lawn chairs while two boys rolled the beer keg toward the opening. "Why the hell did we carry this all the way up here?" one of them asked.

As they crawled out one by one, Polly walked to the boulder where Bridget's oxeye daisies still lay in a heap. Mandy and Bridget stayed behind to pick up plastic cups.

"I'm really sorry, Polly," Mandy said.

Polly nodded. "I know."

꙳ ꙳ ꙳ ꙳

After they'd all gone, Polly took a deep breath. It was another of those illogical things: it was only when she was alone that she stopped feeling alone. Even the larches seemed to agree, giving off a bright white glow and suddenly swaying, like girls who dance only when they're by themselves. If it was weird to love trees this much, then she was weird. She didn't mind it. Like Polly, the larches were outcasts—a conifer that drops its needles, like a cedar but a whole different species. Spectacular, but strange, too.

Polly moved to Baba's tree and sat against the trunk. The ground was bare there; even without its needles, the massive canopy of branches offered protection when it snowed. Leyland Corporation would bring their bulldozers in the spring to carve out their swimming pool; her mother was probably reading Polly's note right now and getting furious all over again; Bree could be miles away or not in the woods at all. But all of that was out there, beyond the span of the larch boughs, beyond the magic of the grove.

Polly closed her eyes, and this time when she opened them she didn't doubt the vision. It was as real as the bristly trunk at her back, as real as the frozen soil beneath her feet. As real, she knew, as she wanted it to be.

The fairy stood by the fire, her wings as red as hot coals. She was Bree, but not Bree. All her beautiful hair had been cut off, her once skull-like features replaced with round cheeks and ruddy skin. She wore a shirt woven of stinging nettles, the prickliest things in the woods, as if she'd wanted to pierce and harden every inch of herself. Beneath the shirt, Polly saw a solid lump the size of a small watermelon where Bree's thin waist had been.

Polly didn't speak. It was like a dream where you can't run or say a word without ruining it. Then she felt a tickle along her shoulder blades, the stroke of a feather across the back of her neck. Something soft but powerful beat against her back, and all the air in the woods seemed to rush in beneath her. Polly felt so dreamy she almost didn't realize what was happening until she lifted off the forest floor, drawn skyward by two slender green wings.

She hovered and gasped for air, hardly believing it. When she stretched her legs and didn't touch the ground, she thought her heart would burst from happiness. She whooped loud enough to startle the forest, but her sister never looked her way. Bree gathered the oxeye daisies, looking plump and sleepy, like a bear ready to bed down for winter. She tucked the leaves against her chest and walked out of the grove.

"Bree!" Polly called, but her sister didn't turn.

This time, Polly wasn't about to let her go. She reached out and all at once she was flying—flitting over the tips of the bare-leafed huckleberry shrubs, up through the black rigging of the larches. Up, up, up to the tops of the trees, where the deep purple sky was just unveiling its stars, and the air was so cold and clean she breathed it in like a mint.

Her heart and wings beat furiously, filling her head with thunder and stirring up windstorms across the crowns of the trees. She saw all the things that were usually hidden, from a raccoon slumbering on a strong branch to a golden eagle's aerie to her sister walking away.

"Bree!" Polly shouted again, but her sister kept walking. Polly feared that she couldn't follow, that once across the border of Girlwood, she would fall from the sky. Her wings quivered, her mouth went dry, but there was only one thing left to do.

She took a deep breath and leaped from the trees. With a

hawklike cry, she spread her wings and flew out of the grove, dodging owls and bats, skimming the highest boughs. Her sister was gone, but in the distance Polly saw a red glow moving through the trees, then floating up to the arms of a fir tree. It paused there for a moment, then winked out, like an eye closing for a long winter's sleep.

Polly hovered in midair, making a choice. Choosing to believe.

"Good night, Bree," she said and beat her wings until she climbed again, soaring up toward Battlecreek Peak. From the ground, she would look like nothing more than a strange cloud or a figment of someone's imagination. "Sleep tight."

꙳ ꙳ ꙳ ꙳

When Polly woke it was pitch-black, and she was alone at the base of Baba's tree. The oxeye daisies were gone, the fire out. She reached behind her and felt only shoulder blades and skin, yet she wasn't disappointed. She still felt light as air.

She walked home under the new-moon sky—huge, black, and crowded with stars. The energy around the trees was white and slowly pulsing, like cold breaths, like sleep.

When she got home, she found her mother on the couch in the living room, Polly's note on the table in front of her. She didn't look panicked or irate, but Polly stayed by the front door, just in case.

Her mom said nothing. Polly's dad was long gone now, and her mom had washed off her makeup. She wore yoga pants and one of Bree's shirts.

Polly felt like a pendulum, swinging one way and then coming back. Growing up, then shrinking to girl size again. Flying away, then flying home. Her mother opened and closed a fist; maybe she felt the same way. Old, then young; mother, then daughter. Dead as winter, then almost shocked when things started growing inside her again.

"Did you see her?" her mom asked.

Polly knew her story would sound like a foolish, childish dream. Like she'd fallen asleep and only imagined her sister there. Of course she hadn't really flown—that was impossible. There were no such things as fairies.

And that's when Polly realized that the hardest thing in the world might very well be to stand alone and believe in something no one else does.

"I saw her," she said. "She took the daisy leaves and left."

Her mother held her gaze, and then began to cry. Not the agonized cries she'd made in Bree's room, but cries of relief.

"Oh, Polly," she said, and Polly raced across the room and into her arms.

19

LARCH

(Larix occidentalis)

*In Siberian mythology, the larch takes the place of
the ash as the World-tree, and burning larch is
said to ward off evil spirits. The spring sap can be
boiled into a syrup to soothe sore throats, the resin
used for bruises and cuts, and the needles and
stems are an antiseptic. An extract from the needles and bark helps emaciated people gain weight.*

*J*ust after dawn, Polly opened her eyes, unsure about what
had woken her. She listened a while, and had almost fallen
back to sleep when she heard footsteps outside, cracking the
ice. She prayed for Bree, but when she ran to her window, she
saw something almost as satisfying. Baba was up again, scat-
tering seeds across the snow.

Polly opened her window. "Baba, what are you doing?"

Her grandmother emptied the last of the seeds from her

pockets and looked up smiling. "Just a little gardening," she said. "You won't know this place in spring."

Polly smiled too, but when her grandmother headed back toward the creek, the grin faded. Baba's rainbow was stunning, but her body looked tiny and frail. She leaned wearily against a tree when she reached the path in the woods.

"Why don't you come in?" Polly called to her. "Say hi to Mom."

But Baba just shook her head and the colors around her shimmered. "I think it's time for me to go home," she said. "Your mother will know I was here."

Polly watched her until she'd disappeared, then headed downstairs. Her mom hadn't cooked much lately, but she was already up making pancakes. Polly didn't give away Baba's secret but sat in the dining room, where the sun streamed in in long, dusty lines. The pancakes were delicious, and as Polly took a second helping, her mom reached into her pocket and took out the lock of charred hair Polly had found in the grove all those months ago.

"The police never tested it," her mother said. "They didn't think it was worthwhile. So I found a lab on my own."

Polly set down her fork, stunned and proud of her mom for risking another heartbreak. She was finally living up to her name: Faith.

"It's hers," her mom said softly. "At least, within the lab's margin of error, it's Bree's hair. And that's enough for me."

They sat in silence as Polly's mom gathered the extra pancakes on a plate.

"We'll leave her more food and blankets," her mother said. "I never told you this, Polly, but that shelter you and the girls made was amazing."

Polly smiled proudly and was about to tell her mom how they'd built it when the doorbell rang. Four months had passed since Bree left, but her mother still raced for the door. There were probably a thousand disappointments coming, but Polly couldn't see any way around that. She'd found Girlwood only after Bree disappeared, and she'd seen Bree only after that horrible party. Maybe the good stuff didn't even register without the bad.

But it wasn't Bree or even Baba at the door. It was Joe Meyer.

"Um," he said. "Can I talk to Polly?"

Polly stood in the dining room in her yellow happy-face pajamas, her hair not as wild as it would have been if she'd left it long, but still a short frizzy nest. She couldn't believe Joe Meyer was standing there, that he even knew where she lived. When he looked around her mother to smile at Polly, it felt like her skin caught fire.

"Of course," her mother said. She raised an eyebrow as she walked to the kitchen, and Polly blushed even redder.

Joe wore a green sweater slightly darker than his eyes and looked so far out of her league it wasn't even funny. "Hey," he said.

"Hey."

He stepped into the entry and closed the door. Joe Meyer was in her house! Polly wished she could call Olivia and tell her.

"Yesterday," he said, then her eyes seemed to freeze him in place. They both stood awkwardly, leaning one way and then the other. She was surprised at his uncertainty. She'd had him pegged as one of those people who always know what to say.

"I'm sorry about the party," he went on at last. "I know that's a special place to you. Carly was all into that swimming pool thing, but on the way back she didn't seem so excited anymore. She was real quiet—spooked or something."

Polly stared at him.

"About this thing with me and Carly," Joe went on, shifting his weight again. "I was amazed when she first went out with me. I wasn't part of that group, you know? I wasn't anybody. I'll admit it was great for a while, being so popular, but then . . . You wouldn't believe some of the stuff they do, the things they say about people. Maybe I should have done something sooner, but last night was the last straw. Carly and I broke up. I wanted you to know."

His words produced the strangest sensation in Polly's chest, as if there were a sparrow inside her flapping its wings.

She was breathing so hard she turned away so he wouldn't think she was having a heart attack.

He cleared his throat. "I thought maybe, you know . . . the mall's open. If you're not busy."

Was he asking her out? Polly expected Carly to burst in laughing at any moment. This had to be a joke. Everyone knew she was the forest freak. Swamp Girl.

"You're not making this easy," Joe said, laughing uncomfortably.

She widened her eyes in surprise. She'd figured her thoughts were as obvious as the happy faces on her pajamas, but maybe Bree had been right when she'd said guys were clueless. Joe might have no idea that right this second she was imagining what it would be like if he kissed her. He might think she was totally indifferent to him, and even though that was a kind of power too, it didn't seem worthy of a girl from Girlwood.

Polly stepped forward, her stomach doing somersaults. "I'm not busy," she said, and smiled.

✳ ✳ ✳ ✳

Polly could have debated endlessly over what clothes Joe might like, but instead she took ten seconds and put on her favorite brown track pants and a cream-colored fleece. Brushing her hair was pointless. Even her short curls were impervious to combs.

Polly's mother offered to drive them the half mile to the mall, but they decided to walk. It was a cold, cloudless morning. The roads had been plowed and the snow piled on the curb like long white hedges. Polly didn't tell him that she hated the mall, all the rock 'n' roll clothes stores and embarrassing Victoria's Secret displays, not to mention the teenagers who shrieked at one another across the atrium as if nobody else existed.

"You need to buy something?" she asked.

"Nah," Joe said, his breath steaming as he spoke. "We'll just hang out. There's nothing else to do. Everybody goes to the Galleria on Saturdays."

Everybody but Polly.

They went quickly through Mervyns and out into the crowded mall. After a loop around the upper floor, all the displays began to look identical to Polly, nothing but headless mannequins in washed-out blue jeans and skimpy shirts.

"Let's go to Caravan," Joe said, and actually took her hand for a moment. The sparrow came back again, banging against Polly's chest. They headed into the store, past a row of crucifixes to the lava lamps and fiber-optic skulls at the back. Joe must have realized it wasn't her thing because he touched her hand again, just for a second, and asked her if she wanted a soft pretzel.

He got himself an Orange Julius and they sat on a bench

overlooking the fountain. A toddler escaped his mother and climbed into the water, grabbing coins. Polly feared Carly or Joy might come along, but no one from school had shown up yet.

Polly's head began to pound. It could have been the smell of bleach or the toddler screaming when his mother picked him up and forced him back into his stroller, but either way she wanted to go home. All of a sudden, it seemed like a test. Could she be a normal girl or not? Could she straighten her hair, get some fashionable clothes, and be likable? Joe had been talking about all the sports he played—track, basketball, karate, football—and now he paused, like she was supposed to list her activities too. Did hiking count? Foraging for food? Flying around the grove?

His smile faded as she remained silent. He looked away and sipped his Orange Julius, then suddenly he turned to face her.

"I'm going to be a research scientist," he said.

That made her sit up. She hadn't figured him for something so ambitious.

"Really?"

"My mom has lupus and I want to discover a drug to cure it. She's pretty much bedridden now."

"I didn't know that. About your mom."

He shrugged. She could see all his freckles again. The sunlight through the atrium must have brought them out.

"It's kind of a sick joke in our house," he said. "I want to make drugs, and my brother, Brad, will be first in line to take them."

Polly squeezed her soft pretzel, amazed that Joe Meyer, of all people, had gone through some of the same things she had.

"Don't get me wrong," he went on. "I love my brother. You'll think this is crazy, but I don't think the guy selling his soul for crystal meth *is* my brother. He's either asleep or in a fog. Lost somewhere, like your sister."

Polly was about to ask him if he thought there was any chance of getting them back when a sharp pain suddenly shot down her leg.

"You okay?" Joe asked.

Polly dropped her pretzel and stood, even though it felt like knife blades from her waist to her feet.

"Polly?" Joe's voice seemed to be coming from far away. "What's wrong?"

She tried to concentrate on his face, but every nerve in her body felt like it was being sliced in half. When her legs gave out, Joe caught her. He eased her back down on the bench as a young mother rushed to get her a cup of water from the drinking fountain. The throbbing eased for a moment, then started up again with a rip. There was a crowd around her now, half a dozen worried faces.

"I have to go," Polly said, struggling to get to her feet again.

"Polly, maybe you should—"

But Polly felt an overwhelming need to run. Despite the pain, she pushed past Joe and raced through the food court, grimacing with every step. She had a hand on the exit door when Joe caught up to her and held her by the shoulders.

"Wait a minute. Just wait! Tell me what's wrong."

Her eyes filled with tears. She knew what the pain meant now. Carly and her father weren't going to wait until spring to cut down the larches. The stabbing in Polly's legs was saw blades, the roaring in her ears the sound of chain saws. Every wizened old tree in Girlwood, including her grandmother's, was coming down.

"The grove," she managed to say. "They're at the grove."

He could have said anything. It was magic when he chose the right words.

"I'm coming with you."

20

OSHA

(*Ligusticum canbyi*)

Osha is named for the Native American word meaning "bear," and it is a sacred healing plant to many tribes. Bears are often spotted eating the plant, presumably for its healing properties. Osha has been used to treat everything from serious respiratory disorders to viral infections to coughs. The entire plant is edible and smells like strong, spicy celery.

*J*oe might have been a track star, but he didn't know the woods the way Polly did. She took every shortcut and easily outpaced him, but even at a dead run she was still too late.

The spiny devil's club, so effective at hiding the grove, had been no match for chain saws. The plant had been obliterated, hacked up into pieces and splayed across the snow, leaving a six-foot-wide opening into Girlwood.

The silence was total. Whoever had been there—Carly or her father or just the hired men with chain saws—was gone, yet Polly couldn't make herself look through that opening. She turned her back to it, like a little kid who thinks she can close her eyes and make the bogeyman disappear.

Joe came charging out of the pines, shattering the quiet. He took one look at the remains of the grove and said, "Maybe you shouldn't go in."

Polly squared her shoulders and turned around. Even before she saw the damage, she noticed the sky—a wide expanse of blue where there had been only green before. She squinted into the empty brightness, then slowly lowered her gaze. No tree had been spared. Every last larch had been sliced off at the stump and dropped unceremoniously in a tangled heap. Bridget's shelter had been crushed, and the boulder where they'd left food for Bree was buried six trunks deep. The air smelled of gasoline.

"Oh" was all Polly could say.

She didn't realize Joe was beside her until he squeezed her arm. Time stopped, and she couldn't get it going again. She was stuck in the worst moment, replaying it over and over, the way her mother had been stuck in the day Bree left.

"I don't think Carly wanted *this*," Joe said quietly.

Polly squeezed her eyes shut. It didn't matter what Carly wanted. The damage was done. Polly tried to picture the grove the way it had been, but even her imagination had been hacked up. She couldn't see Girlwood any way but ruined.

She opened her eyes, willing back tears. She clambered over the mounds of trunks, wanting to identify each fallen tree individually—the sapling that had always been a bit of a rebel, standing alone near the devil's club; the ones that used to hog the sunlight; the shadow lovers with their coats of furry moss. She wouldn't stop until she found them all.

Joe didn't ask what she was doing. He merely helped her drag away debris. After nearly an hour of digging through the wreckage, Polly finally came to the massive trunk of Baba's tree.

She touched the wood and used every bit of imagination she had to see it still standing—its trunk ramrod straight and unyielding, its branches laden with feathery needles, its canopy so wide it blocked the sun. Instead of shocked silence, she pretended there was a whistle of wind still blowing through the tree's branches and the scrabbling of squirrels up the weathered bark.

She smiled a little, imagining what those tiny feet and claws would feel like on her own skin, the weight of a crow on her shoulder, a robin coiling her hair into a nest. She closed her eyes and pictured her feet as roots and the comforting feel of cool earth around her ankles. As the skin on her arms turned brown and crinkly, her fingers curled upward, straining for the sky.

She imagined the cycles of snow and rain, heat and fire,

cooling winds and winter's chill once again. She told time in seasons, in the moon's three faces, in the hawks born in her branches and the bears who died at her feet.

Polly stroked Baba's tree and pictured even stranger things. A grizzled man's face—one she'd seen only in a photograph on Baba's dresser—and a wild garden. A daughter, then the daughter's children. Herself and Bree, scampering through the woods.

Polly opened her eyes, one word tearing at her throat.

"Baba," she said.

❧ ❧ ❧ ❧

She left Joe and ran, but once again, she was not quick enough.

Baba sat in her garden, her back against the trunk of the purple ash. Baba had once told Polly that an ash in the garden is like a larch in the woods. Both trees of life, passageways between worlds.

"Baba!" Polly cried.

Polly fell to her knees in the snow beside her grandmother. Baba's eyes were half closed, her breathing labored. The rainbow now streamed from her body up the trunk of the ash, staining the brown bark violet and yellow and green.

Baba moistened her lips, trying to speak. "Don't . . . be scared."

But Polly was terrified. She'd proven she could live without a lot of things: without popularity and her dad, without Olivia and Bree, even without the grove. But she could not live without her grandmother, the one person who looked at her, always, as if she was exactly as she should be. And worse than that, Polly knew Bree couldn't survive without Baba either.

Her grandmother's breathing turned raspier, more like a gurgle than a breath.

"Baba?" Polly cried. "Have you tried the osha? Remember that sick bear who ate it and got better?"

As Baba's eyes began to close, Polly squeezed her hand. "Tell me what to do," Polly pleaded. "Please! Even with the snow, I can find any plant you need. I can do it now. Just tell me what you need."

Her grandma opened her eyes. It seemed to take all her energy to do it, as if she were lifting a hundred-pound weight.

"I . . . loved to walk," Baba said.

A wail escaped Polly's lips. There had to be something in her grandmother's kitchen that would help; if not osha, then heal-all or lichen. A magic plant, a spell. It was unbearable to think that some things were beyond fixing. Beyond magic. Beyond what even Baba could do.

"I walked everywhere I needed to go," Baba continued, her voice such a whisper Polly had to lean close to hear. "Some people go all over the world to find what they're looking for, but everything I needed was right here. Did you know—"

She coughed, and when blood came up, Polly whimpered. She pulled a sodden leaf from the snow and dabbed her grandmother's chin.

"Grandma."

"I saw every plant that grows here," Baba said. "Even one your mother would like. It's probably got some official name, but I called it Faith. It's a tiny blue thing that blooms in the grove in April. You should show it to her."

"Please don't go," Polly said. "Bree . . . we both need you."

She was close enough that Baba could place a kiss right on her cheek. "Oh, Polly," she said. "Don't worry. It's been a joy."

"I'm sorry I didn't protect the grove. I should have—"

Her grandma shushed her. "Don't be silly. I'm so proud of you."

Polly rested her head against her grandmother's chest. As long as she was listening to Baba's heart beating, she thought, it couldn't stop. Yet the colors around Baba also vied for her attention. Only a thread clung to Baba now, while the rest of the arc hopped from limb to limb like some crazy tropical bird. Even through her tears, Polly had to smile. Baba herself had always paused to look at anything out of the ordinary, from rainbows to exotic mushrooms to the people who dared to come to her door. Every day has a moment of wonder in it, she'd once said to Polly, that most people pass right by.

The rainbow twirled and hopped and finally leaped from the ash to the first pine in the woods, forming a perfect jewel-toned horseshoe, arcs of garnet and sapphire, ruby and emerald, amethyst and pearl. Then, finally spreading itself too thin, the rainbow snapped. For a moment, the whole world was splashed with color, and then normal daylight returned, muted and gray.

Polly pressed her ear firmly against her grandmother's chest, but she no longer heard a heartbeat. Polly began to shudder, and for once she didn't try to act brave or stop her weeping. She cried so hard, even Olivia would have been impressed. Her wailing must have led Joe right to her, because at some point he pulled her away from Baba and took her in his arms.

Her whole body shook, and she couldn't imagine it ever stopping. Without Baba, the world was an unsteady place. She expected Joe to pull away, to grow tired of her sobbing, but he held on silently until her tears quieted to hiccups. Then he reached into his pocket and took out a larch branch he'd brought from the grove, laying the tiny limb on her grandmother's lap.

Even through her tears, Polly could see that his spirit was brown, like her father's, but on Joe it was most prominent near his feet. When he stayed very still, thin roots stretched from his soles into the earth, and eventually Polly felt them beneath her, slow, soothing pulses through the soil. Every day has a moment of wonder in it.

Baba, she thought, would have liked him.

21

EVENING PRIMROSE
(Oenothera)

Evening primrose is entirely edible: the leaves and flowers are delicious in salads, the seedpods can be steamed and the roots cooked like potatoes. Medicinally, the bark and leaves are useful in the treatment of whooping cough and asthma, and an oil from the seeds may help prevent cirrhosis, rheumatoid arthritis, and multiple sclerosis.

*O*ne Babaism was that there was not much difference between people and plants: both do better with a little tending, both turn toward the sun, both grow tougher over time, and both die. Life works like a garden, Baba liked to say—not in a straight line, but in cycles of growth, death, and rebirth. If the summer harvest goes bad, it's no cause for worry. Come spring, you get to start all over again.

Bree might have declared all Babaisms nonsense, but Polly

and her parents had proved that this one, at least, was true. They'd survived Bree's loss, started to go on without her, then circled around to mourning again. The only difference was that this time it was Baba herself whom they'd lost.

Polly lay on her bed listening to her parents' muffled voices downstairs. She'd stopped crying, but her brain was slow. She couldn't recall what had happened after Baba died. She knew Joe had run to get her father and that the three of them had taken Baba's body inside her house. But after Joe left, things got fuzzy. She couldn't remember what her father had said, how they'd gotten home, or even what her mother's reaction to the news of Baba's death had been.

Her father's voice suddenly boomed through the floor-boards, the way it always did when he was on the phone. Since he'd moved to his cabin, he could no longer understand technology, anything that didn't live and breathe.

"I'm calling to get some information on your cemetery plots," he shouted. "Do you handle the casket as well?"

Polly battled her way through the numbness. A casket? A cemetery in the middle of town? She pushed herself off the bed, her legs weak and tingly as she hurried downstairs. In the kitchen, her father leaned wearily against the counter, the phone in his hand. Her mother sat at the table, her eyes red but dry.

"You're not burying Baba in town, are you?" Polly said. "We've got to bring her back to the grove!"

Her father put his hand over the phone. "Polly, please," he said. "Go back to bed. Your mother and I—"

"You can't let someone take her body!" Polly whirled on her mother. "What if they bury her where there aren't any trees?"

Her mom went pale; someone's voice came through the phone, asking if anyone was still there.

Polly's dad turned his attention back to the phone. "Can I call you back?" he shouted. "My daughter is a little upset."

As he hung up, Polly put her hands on her hips. She was stunned at how quickly the feeling in her legs had come back, at how strong she could be without Baba behind her.

"Polly," her dad began, but she was already shaking her head.

"Don't tell me about the rules," Polly said. "I don't care what you're supposed to do now. All that matters is what's *right*. Baba belongs in that grove."

Her dad looked at her like she was crazy, but her mom got to her feet. Faith Greene's reflection in the window was a pale, wide-eyed version of herself, and Polly realized that although she had lost her grandmother, her mother had lost her last parent. Polly didn't even want to imagine how that felt.

"You know it, Mom," Polly said softly. "That's her place. We have to take her back."

"That's Dan Leyland's property, Polly," her mom said, not turning from the window.

"No, it's not," Polly replied. "You can't own the woods."

Her mother stepped away from her reflection and touched Polly's arm. Polly expected a long-winded rational argument about the things you could and could not do, but her mom surprised her by smiling.

"That's exactly what Baba would have said."

Her dad stepped forward. "Don't tell me you're actually considering this."

Polly was glad for her mother's hand on her arm, holding her steady while everything in their house turned around.

"Polly's right," her mom said. "My mother belongs in the grove."

"You can't be serious! You can't just bury a body on someone else's property. There are procedures, Faith. There has to be a coroner's report, papers, a death certificate. I suppose after all that, we could have her cremated and sprinkle—"

"No. She'd want her bones there," Polly's mom said. She was quiet a moment, thinking, then she looked up, her eyes twinkling like Baba's.

"We could tell everybody she's out walking," she said. "She's gone away for long periods before. When she doesn't come back, people will say what they always have: that wolves got her. That she's still walking somewhere, lost in her plants, and is never coming back." She turned to Polly. "You'd have to talk to Joe. He'd have to lie, Polly. He couldn't tell anyone that he was with you when . . . she died. Would he do that?"

Polly's dad looked at them as if they'd lost their minds, but Polly smiled. "I think so."

Her mom rubbed her forehead, the twinkle in her eyes turning to tears.

"Mom?" Polly said. "Are you sure? Because if people find out, they'll think—"

"To hell with what people think," her mother said. Then she looked back toward the window and, at last, put her head in her hands and cried.

The grove was a fitting graveyard. It was terrible to go back.

The larches still lay in ignoble heaps, awaiting logging trucks and a ride to the paper mill. With the trees down, the borders of Girlwood had been revealed. Polly was stunned at how small the grove really was—just a few dozen yards across. Why had it seemed so vast and impenetrable before? They'd been deceived by shadows and branches. As long as there had been trees in their way, they could imagine a million possibilities for what lay beyond them.

Despite the snow on the ground and the ominous storm clouds, Polly's dad was down to short sleeves. He'd chosen a spot for the grave well beyond the location of the future swimming pool and had been digging through frozen soil all night. It was backbreaking work, and no one but Polly's father could have done it.

"I'll go down to her house and get her," he said. "I'll have to make sure I'm not seen, so it might be a while."

Polly's mom reached for his hand, and it was only then that his shoulders sank from weariness. Polly wished for a tree to hide behind so that they could forget about her. Instead, her dad climbed over a fallen trunk and left the grove.

Polly could no longer see a glow around the debris. Only her mother's aura lit up the grove—not a wavering candle flame but a steady white glow, as if she were taking over where Baba had left off.

The bow and drill were buried somewhere, so Polly started from scratch. She searched the piles of debris for the right pieces to make a bow and spindle. Her mother watched Polly silently as she notched a fireboard, strung the bow with her shoelace, then began the quick sawing motion to create a coal. When she had the ember, she transferred it carefully to a heap of needles, blowing gently to spark a flame. Her mother looked at her as if she'd never seen her before.

"I never knew you could do that," she said quietly as she held her hands over the fire.

"Baba taught me," Polly said proudly, fighting tears.

The larch wood sent up flames of lavender and green. It was a good hour before Polly's dad came back, trudging up the mountain with Baba in his arms. Without her towering spirit, she looked tiny, like a sleeping child. Polly's dad laid her out gently in the grave.

Then they looked at one another, and Polly realized neither of her parents knew what to do next. A few months ago, this would have stunned and alarmed her, but today Polly merely stepped forward. Her grandmother's favorite song came back to her in its entirety, as if Baba had lent her her own voice.

Honey, child, honey, child, whither are you going?
Would you cast your jewels all to the breezes blowing?
Would you leave the mother who on golden grain has fed you?
Would you grieve the lover who is riding forth to wed you?

Mother mine, to the wild forest I am going,
Where upon the champa boughs the champa buds are blowing;
To the koil-haunted river-isles where lotus lilies glisten,
The voices of the fairy folk are calling me: O listen!

Honey, child, honey, child, the world is full of pleasure,
Of bridal-songs and cradle-songs and sandal-scented leisure.
Your bridal robes are in the loom, silver and saffron glowing,
Your bridal cakes are on the hearth: O whither are you going?

The bridal-songs and cradle-songs have cadences of sorrow,
The laughter of the sun to-day, the wind of earth to-morrow.
Far sweeter sound the forest-notes where forest-streams are
*   falling;*
O mother mine, I cannot stay, the fairy-folk are calling.

Polly's mom stared at her, glowing like the moon, then finally kissed her head. Each of them scooped up a handful of cold earth and threw it over the grave, but before they could shovel in the rest of the dirt, there were voices over the ridge. Polly's eyes burned with fury and frustration. They couldn't be found out!

The voices got closer, and Polly's mom strode across the grove. But it wasn't Dan Leyland or some graveyard police whom she confronted by the remains of the devil's club. It was only Joe. And John and Peter. And Mandy and Bridget and Olivia. Each carried a larch seedling in a brown paper bag.

"Don't worry," Joe said immediately. "We swore each other to secrecy. But we're your friends, Polly. We needed to come."

Polly blinked, not to stop her tears but to be sure that what she saw was real. She had friends, real, devoted friends. Friends who would try to stitch her heart back together if it broke, friends who brought *trees*, friends who wouldn't laugh when she told them their spirits had sprouted wings. Pointed and raven black along Bridget's back, shimmering like blue fins between Mandy's shoulder blades, moth brown and unassuming on Joe's spine. Aquamarine and quick-beating around Peter, slow and shell-like for John, thick and bushy on Olivia. *They* were the magic, the fairies. It was real life, not some bedtime story, that was enchanted.

"I told my mom what happened to the grove," Olivia said.

"I don't know if it changed her mind about you and me, but she did say that I could come here and bring this." She held up her larch seedling. "The man at the forest nursery thought we were crazy. He said no one plants this time of year, but we had to try."

It began to snow while they planted. Mandy used the embers from Polly's fire to melt the ground; Bridget dug down deep near the last of the devil's club; Olivia, Joe, and the boys planted their seedlings in the soft soil around the grave. Their beating wings kept the snow out of their eyes, though they mistook it for the breeze. As soon as Polly's dad filled in the grave, snow began to cover it.

"It's almost as if . . ." he began, then turned away, reluctant to finish.

But Polly smiled anyway. Almost as if Baba had sent her own blizzard and was watching her gravesite disappear with a laugh.

🌿 🌿 🌿 🌿

For the next six weeks, the snows kept coming. The local weathercasters said they'd never seen anything like it. Winter started late, then wouldn't stop. Dan Leyland gave an interview to the *Laramie Bee* and said he was ready to start construction on Mountain Winds the moment the ground thawed.

He'd already downed the trees on the site of the community swimming pool and would remove the timber at the first sign of spring.

Life didn't stop in winter, but in Laramie it looked like it did. Neighbors drew the blinds and turned up their televisions, ignoring the weather until it was hospitable again. Even Polly placed the last of the jars of green beans in the woods but didn't go back to check if the food had been taken. She was thirteen now, and it wasn't so horrible Facing Facts. It didn't have to mean the worst would happen—it only meant admitting that it was winter and she had done all she could. Either Bree would survive, or she wouldn't. Polly knew now that she and Baba had never been the ones keeping Bree alive. From the start, the only person who could save Bree was herself.

Polly and her mother spent their evenings going through Baba's cottage, sifting through the dirt on the closet floor that looked almost like a garden bed, picking out seeds and roots from every drawer. Her house had always been more outside than in. In the only bureau Baba hadn't burned in her last bonfire, they found a wooden jewelry box full of vials of primrose oil, which Baba had used to cure everything from asthma to arthritis, and beneath the vials a baby picture of Bree. Polly's mom took out the photo, stroking her finger over the image as if she was brushing back Bree's hair.

"I sometimes think Bree came to her," she said. "Maybe my mother protected her, tucked her away in some shelter and kept her safe. Could Baba have kept something like that from me?"

Her gaze burned into Polly, as if her greatest wish were that her own mother had lied to her. Polly wasn't sure what to think: the place between her mother and grandmother was still a no-woman's-land, but something had taken root in the soil anyway.

"If it had been me," Polly said, "I'd have gone to Baba."

Polly's mom sighed and slid the picture of Bree into her pocket. Then she handed the jewelry box with its valuable oils to Polly.

"She'd want you to have it," she said.

꒜ ꒜ ꒜ ꒜

After that, Polly's mom went into the Crying Room only once, on Bree's seventeenth birthday. She started going out with friends again, and on a Friday in late February, she went to dinner with Polly's dad. This time, there was no premature talk of working things out. They stammered like teenagers just saying hello, yet the next week he arrived on their doorstep to take her out again.

By March, when Bree had been gone six months, Polly's

mom and dad were officially dating, and Polly seesawed between hopefulness and total embarrassment when she stumbled upon them kissing on the porch. She did like the little carvings her dad brought, though, miniature wooden polar bears and log cabins and wolves. Polly's mom put them on the mantel, and even though her dad still lived at his cabin, the house filled up with the scent of wood. After that, somehow, it was easier to sleep.

It was true that sometimes winter felt like it would never end, but it was also the season of dreaming. Polly burrowed under her covers and dreamed of hibernating fairies, of bear dens and the roots of those larch seedlings taking hold in black, cold soil.

She lay in bed and thought that at thirteen she was just beginning to understand the secret of survival: when things are at their darkest, just take a deep breath and wait.

22

FIREWEED
(GREAT WILLOW-HERB)
(*Epilobium angustifolium*)

*An earth regenerator, fireweed got its name because it is
often the first to grow in burned and clear-cut areas,
springing up through the ash after Mount Saint Helens
exploded, and amid the rubble of bombed cities. When
young, the whole vitamin-rich plant can be eaten like
asparagus, and when used in teas, fireweed is a remedy
for asthma.*

$\mathscr{P}$olly's mom liked to say there were four seasons in Idaho:
fire, winter, more winter, and mud. The mud came in late
March, after days of steady downpours. Afternoons flirted
with the fifty-degree mark, yet most people stayed inside as
if it were still winter, standing at their windows and cursing
the slop in their yards.

Only Bridget cheered the clouds. To her, every rainstorm
slowed construction at Mountain Winds and gave her the op-
portunity to gather the Kids for the Woods at the Leyland

Corporation's construction office. On a miserable, wet Saturday, Dan Leyland drove up with Carly in the seat beside him to find twenty thirteen-year-olds picketing around his silent bulldozers and chanting, "Stop Mountain Winds."

"Now, now," Mr. Leyland said, stepping out of his mud-splattered truck wearing jeans and a cowboy hat. Carly got out after him, already dressed for next season in white boots and a miniskirt. "That's enough. You've made your point."

"Mr. Leyland," Bridget said, "we have a right to voice our opinion. We think—"

"I know what you think," he said, looking at her from under the brim of his hat. "You think I have no soul. You think I'm just a businessman and all I care about is money and progress. But you're wrong. I believe in protecting natural spaces too."

Polly rolled her eyes, wishing her friends could see his comic-book-pink aura.

"Why do you think I'm taking on this project?" he went on. "I'm not making much of a profit, I can tell you that. I'm doing it so people will have access to wilderness. You want to save your precious woods? You've got to let people in to see them. No one's going to protect what they don't know."

The only sound was the steady rain until Peter mumbled that Mr. Leyland made a good point. Polly was outraged and about to offer a rebuttal when Carly suddenly stepped forward, her white boots disappearing into a murky puddle.

"That's not true," Carly said.

Her dad had been turning to leave, but now he stiffened. "Excuse me?"

Under his steady gaze, Carly's aura went from a fireworks display to a flicker, but more surprisingly, the colors around her began to deepen. Those baby blues and pinks became richer hues of turquoise and red, and maybe they colored her vision too because when she looked at the Kids for the Woods, it was as if she'd never seen them before.

"That's not true about your profit," Carly said, her voice soft but firm. "I heard you tell Mom you stand to make well over a million when all is said and done."

Everyone was silent, then Bridget lifted her sign and began the chant again. "Stop Mountain Winds! Stop Mountain Winds!" Dan Leyland glared at her, not about to change his plans just because his daughter had learned to stand up to him, yet obviously unsettled. And Polly couldn't help but wonder if before Girlwood was ruined, it had worked a bit of magic on Carly Leyland, too.

Carly's dad grabbed the picket right out of Bridget's hand, silencing her. "Get off my property," he said, "before I call the police."

✿ ✿ ✿ ✿

The moment the ground was dry, Dan Leyland put his men on twelve-hour shifts. Polly and her mother waited anxiously the day the trees were removed from Girlwood, but if the crew noticed the larch seedlings or Baba's grave, there was no report of it. With the weather finally cooperating, trucks moved in, and bulldozers attacked the woods and newly green fields. Everywhere Polly turned there were downed trees and daffodils, both reminders that spring had come but Bree had not.

On a warm Sunday afternoon, Polly's mom drove past the newly completed waterfall at the entrance to Mountain Winds. Through the open window, Polly smelled chlorine and saw the pennies that had been tossed into the concrete-lined pond. There were red and green banners now, and a dozen FOR SALE signs along with waterproof boxes of brochures.

Her mother reached over and squeezed her hand. "I'm sorry, honey."

Polly said nothing. Today, at least, she wasn't going to think about Mountain Winds. For the moment, all that mattered was that her mother had asked to see her father's cabin for the first time. They were going to spend the day together as a family in the woods.

A mile beyond the subdivision, they reached the turnoff, a weedy dirt trail that Polly had to insist was the road. Muttering "Crazy fool" under her breath, her mother eased off the pavement, wincing as the thistle and switchgrass scraped the underbelly of her car.

Twice, Polly had to get out and move rocks from the path, but finally they reached the cozy woodman's cottage that looked, as always, like a holdover from another time. As they pulled up near the shed, Polly and her mother saw it at the same time—the girl on the porch beside her father, carved from larch.

Polly's mom didn't move. The carving was so lifelike that, with only a little stretch of the imagination, they could think that it was Bree standing there and that, like magic, their family was once again whole. Polly didn't want to believe that this was the best they would get, a wooden statue of her sister, but if it was, she knew they could survive it. It seemed cruel to go on, but it was right, too. As if they were truly creatures of the wild now, the kind who persevered.

Her mom surprised her by throwing open the door and running to Polly's dad.

"Oh, Paul," she said. "She's beautiful."

Polly left them to the carving and headed down to the stream. The construction sounds were louder there, a chorus of rumbles and shrieks. Polly picked up rocks and threw them into the churning river. With the snowmelt and heavy rains, the water had never been as deep.

Later, her mom walked down from the cabin. Polly had thought her mother's aura was pure white, but lately she'd noticed flecks of green and blue in it, as if she was slowly letting color back in.

"This place is ridiculous," her mom said. "Who lives like this? No electricity. No microwave or TV. Not even a phone!" But when she glanced back at the cabin, her gaze softened. "And yet, this'll sound crazy—"

"I don't need TV," Polly said quickly, her heart pounding. She'd never dared to ask for this. To live *here*. In the woods.

"It's like another world. A refuge. Maybe . . ." Her mother looked over the river, then stepped out onto a partially submerged rock. Polly could hardly believe the sight of her mom balancing there, letting the icy water slosh over the rims of her tennis shoes. For a moment, she looked trapped, unable to chance another step forward but too far out to go back. Then she suddenly jumped across the deepest water and landed on the other side with a *splat*.

"Did you see that?" her mom asked, her eyes shining.

What Polly saw was that her mom was growing out her hair. And walking. Not as far as Baba had, but around the block some evenings, to the store and back.

"Maybe we could come here on the weekends," her mom said. "You know, just to see how it feels. The only thing is, do you think Bree would find us?"

Polly took the same path across the river, ignoring the water that seeped into her shoes. "Of course she will," she said, adding the rest silently. *If she can.*

Her mom squeezed her hand. "Let's go for a walk."

They headed into the tidied forest which, to Polly's mind, was no longer a forest at all. The Leyland Corporation had removed all the underbrush, leaving the ground oddly clean and bare. Even the firs had been trimmed into perfect-looking Christmas trees, without a single dead branch to mar their appeal. Polly shook her head and led her mom down where the forest had yet to be "fixed," into the overgrown canyon where the river raged and Mandy had caught her fish.

It was a hard hike through tangles of barbed hawthorns and across the snowy patches on the north slope. Ahead was the steep, exposed hill that led up to Girlwood, the summit painfully barren since the crews had removed every last larch.

Polly suddenly turned, nearly knocking her mother over.

"It's April!" she said. "I completely forgot. Baba said there was a flower you'd like in the grove. A blue one that blooms this month. We have to find it."

She looked up the cliff, longing to go back to Girlwood but terrified of what she would find. What if the larch seedlings her friends had planted had all died?

"Hardly anything's in bloom, honey," her mom said. "We'll come back later."

"No!"

Polly's body was covered in goose bumps, the same feeling

she'd always had in the grove. Only the frost-hardy glacier lilies were in bloom at this elevation, yet she knew she had to find that flower.

"Come on," Polly said, looking for a place to cross the river. But all through the canyon the water was fast and deep, the edges still locked in ice.

"We can't cross here, Polly," her mom said. "If you're so determined, we can go back to the cabin and drive around. This makes no sense."

Polly looked at the churning water. Of course her mom was right, but right didn't explain her goose bumps. Right had nothing to do with the furious beating of her heart.

"Baba named it Faith," she said. "The flower."

Her mom looked stunned for a moment, then she let out a grudging laugh. "She always knew just how to get to me, didn't she?"

Polly smiled, leading her mother where the river was narrowest and praying that the fast current wouldn't sweep them off their feet.

"Aaaaah," her mom said as they stepped into the icy water. "This had better be one good-looking flower." Battling the current and the slick rocks, they shuffled and stumbled their way across. Polly's jeans became a lead weight as she broke the ice on the far side and pulled her mother out after her.

"I can't feel my toes," her mom said.

Polly looked up the steep cliff, fearing that her mother wouldn't be able to climb it. Then she realized she wouldn't have to.

Just a few feet above them, nestled between two sheltering rocks, was a tiny speck of blue. Polly scrambled upward, expecting something wondrous and strange, a flower that reminded her of Baba, then sank to her knees in disappointment beside the tiny bud. The flower was nothing but six cobalt petals and a fuzzy pinkish stem. It was a true blue, and that was rare, but otherwise it was just an ordinary spring flower. Something most people would walk right by.

Sighing, her mother clambered up the slope and knelt beside her. She acted amazed and impressed, just like she had when Polly was little and proudly offered her a terrible finger painting for the refrigerator. Her mom even put her head down to the ground to see the flower's underside.

"Maybe it's better when more are in bloom," Polly said, looking up the cliff. It glowed blue already and soon would be covered with blossoms. It would be pretty, Polly was certain, but hardly worth the effort of hiking all the way here.

Polly's mom caught her arm. "I've never seen this before," she said.

Polly drew back. "What do you mean? You know all the plants around here."

Her mom shook her head. "Obviously not, because I've

never seen this one. Not in all my fieldwork. Not in any book."

Polly looked at the tiny flower. *Faith.* The goose bumps became a full-blown chill.

"Do you know what that means?" her mom went on, looking at the hundreds of fuzzy pink stems just beginning to push through the soil. "If it grows only here? On this slope, in your grove?"

Polly was almost afraid to say it, afraid she'd jinx it. But then she thought of her friends and Baba and the short but magical season they'd all spent in Girlwood, and decided that nothing was too good to be true.

"It means you'll need to change your report," Polly said, "and say there's something worthwhile in the woods after all." Her mother stared at her, and Polly began to smile.

❧ ❧ ❧ ❧

As far as the botanists could tell, the flower grew only in the woods around Laramie, in the desolate, rocky soil where nothing else could thrive.

Those damn flowers, Dan Leyland called the new discovery. *Glaucanula parvifolius*, otherwise known as Faith. During the last days of April, they came up everywhere on his land. A judge ordered a midnight injunction, halting all construction until an investigation of the flower's range and habitat could be completed. Dan Leyland hired a team of fancy lawyers to counterattack, but for the moment, *Glaucanula parvifolius,* Faith, looked like an endangered species. There wasn't a thing Mr. Leyland or anyone could do until someone figured out how to protect it.

Polly was thrilled to learn that a tiny flower, the smallest thing, had that much power. Anything could happen at the end of the legal battle, but for now the bulldozers remained silent. In a fit of spite, Dan Leyland marched to the Mountain Winds entrance and turned off the waterfall.

It was all anyone could talk about. Some people argued for the Leylands, saying it was insane to stop a multimillion-dollar project for one little plant, but others rallied around the woods now that something rare and valuable had been found there. People argued about Baba, too. Some said her heart must have given out on a walk through the woods; others suggested that wolves had gotten her. In any case, now that the worst threat had vanished, Olivia's mom softened her stance about Polly. She even drove Olivia out to the cabin one weekend, letting the girls spend their first afternoon together in weeks.

Polly's mom said they could take a walk as long as they stuck to the trails they knew. Olivia and Polly looked at each other, then immediately began gathering spring beauties.

Polly hadn't been back to Girlwood since they'd buried Baba, but now, with Olivia beside her, she knew it was time.

As they approached the grove, though, Polly had second thoughts. When she caught a glimpse of the bright sky and the barren place where the devil's club had been, she looked away.

"Let's go back, Olivia," she said. "Please."

Olivia walked forward alone. "Oh, Polly. It's all right. Look."

Reluctantly, Polly turned back and followed her. Crossing the old borders of Girlwood, so much had changed it was hard to make sense of what she saw. The sky was still too bright, and no traces remained of the giant larches, but along the ground something else had come to life. Polly knelt down and brushed her fingers across a carpet of red and blue blossoms. Faith had sprung up everywhere, along with fireweed, a plant that thrived in clear-cuts and burn sites, in the very places where all hope seemed to be lost. And somewhere beneath the vibrant flowers and stalks lay Baba's grave, forever hidden, the larch seedlings Polly's friends had planted around it already two feet tall.

Polly laughed in relief and threw her arms around Olivia, then set out the spring beauties on a rock. All afternoon, they lay among the flowers and talked of which larch seedlings would become the sides to another shelter, of how Girlwood would look in ten years, in twenty, in the year when they brought their own daughters to see it. It was only when the light got dim that they started down the mountain, and almost immediately Olivia tugged her sleeve. Joe Meyer was coming up the path, the way he frequently did on weekends. He visited Polly so often, everyone assumed he was her boyfriend, but Polly couldn't tell. It burned her up at night, wondering if he'd ever kiss her, if he was even thinking about it, or if he only thought of her as a friend.

"You guys are so dumb," Olivia said.

Polly turned to her, ready to argue, but Olivia was laughing. "Even I can see how much he likes you."

Joe paused in the path. Maybe he'd heard Olivia. And maybe Polly didn't care. She walked toward him quickly and kissed him before she could talk herself out of it. For a moment, it was her worst nightmare—him just standing there, shell-shocked, not kissing her back. Then he touched the curls on her neck that she still cut herself and pulled her toward him. She felt him smiling beneath the kiss, and she smiled too.

Joe held her hand as the three of them walked back to the cabin, and Polly realized there was no denying it. Spring was everywhere—in the sprawling patch of miner's lettuce in the meadow and the strange and potent herbs that had come up in their yard. And there, on the front porch of the cabin, in the ragged-haired girl with one hand on her bulging belly and the other drawing away from the door, as if she was afraid to knock.

Polly's heart leaped as she recognized the turtleneck she'd left for Bree in Girlwood all those months ago, as her sister turned to meet her gaze at last.

"Bree!" Polly shouted, and began to run. Even with the wind in her ears, and Joe and Olivia running beside her, she heard her mother's cry in the cabin and the pounding of her father's footsteps across the floor. "Bree."

Author's Note

Dear Readers,

I truly believe, as Polly does, that it is real life and not some bedtime story that is enchanted. Magic is everywhere, all the time. An example of that is the energy field around all living creatures—the aura, or light—that Polly sees.

You might be surprised to know that auras are real, and Polly's gift for seeing them is not unusual. These energy fields come in all shapes and colors, and with a little practice, you can see them too. The first step is to get a partner, or stand in front of a mirror. The background should be blank and preferably white. To see the aura, look about two inches away from your partner's (or your) body at the wall. Let your eyes relax into that area the way you'd relax into a hidden 3-D image. Don't look at the body; look beyond it. The aura should appear. Most people have no trouble seeing a narrow band of white light around others, but seeing colors takes more time and patience. According to many experts, different-colored auras mean different things. Purple, for instance, means you are sensitive, artistic, and idealistic. People with green auras are helpful, strong, and friendly. For more information on aura colors and their meanings, along with a quiz to help you discover your own aura color, see my website: www.clairedean.net.

Another real-life wonder can be found wherever wild things still grow. I am fortunate enough to have a rustic cabin much like Polly's father's—no electricity, lots of towering pines, water brought in from a stream—where I can forage for and eat many of the same plants Polly discovered near Girlwood. Fireweed (delicious!) and mallow (yes, it *does* taste somewhat like cheese), serviceberries and the red, cucumber-tasting berries of twisted stalk, goldenrod leaves (a little chewy) and a scrumptious chickweed salad. Every time I bring home a basket of wild food, I feel capable and strong. It is empowering to be able to take care of myself and my family, at least for one meal! But because edible plants often have poisonous look-alikes and no plant should ever be eaten without one-hundred-percent positive identification, it is essential to use a good field guide. Living in the West, I use *Edible and Medicinal Plants of the West* by Gregory L. Tilford. For more information, see my website or find a field guide that focuses on your area.

It was a joy to create a place as magical as Girlwood, but to my mind real life is far more wonderful and mysterious. Get out into nature. Take a moment to look at the aura around your friends, your pets, even the trees in your yard. The whole world, including you, shimmers.

Best wishes,
Claire Dean